T0151884

Chance

CHANCE

a novel

Steve Shilstone

BREAKAWAY BOOKS
NEW YORK CITY
1996

Chance
© 1996 by Steve Shilstone

ISBN: 1-55821-450-X
Library of Congress Catalog Card Number: 95-83175

Published by:
BREAKAWAY BOOKS
P. O. Box 1109
Ansonia Station
New York, NY 10023
(212) 595-2216

Breakaway Books are distributed by Lyons & Burford,
Publishers, 31 West 21st Street, New York, NY 10010.

FIRST EDITION

Chance

① Hello

Okay, here's the deal. This is a book about a baseball player. Do you care? If you don't care, read it anyway. There's some other stuff in it, too. Chance Caine. Recognize the name? Well, he wants me, an old weird guy poet, to write his story. Why? I'll tell you why. He has made rhythmic marks on paper himself. Some of his efforts aren't even dreck. You can judge for yourself in a minute. He took a class. I gave him an A. So one day he comes to me with a load of scrapbooks, diaries, videos. He says, "Here's my life. How would you like to write my book?" I say, "The thing I make will be the thing I make." I talk like that on purpose sometimes. Art is a conscious attempt at nonverbal communication. Okay? Okay. I lie to convey truth. I lie to make the story better. I am a lying guy. What can I say? I want to write this story. There may be money in it. Why lie? Okay, there's another reason. I gave my students an assignment to write a short short short story no longer than ten sentences. Mr. Caine wrote:

The Angry Fish

The fish hurled himself into the boat slashing left and right with fins, teeth, and daggers. Blood spurted from the severed limbs of the screaming crew. The fish turned a final somersault, stood on its tail on the rail, and shreiked in trembling rage, "Vengeance is mine, haa ha haaa ha! ! !" Then he dove under the waves and was gone.

THE END

What the??? I graded it A and from then on leaned back a little in my chair when he walked by. I leaned back further after I had read his science fiction slash fantasy effort a few weeks later. You'll see that one, too, in time. Who is this guy? Let's see if I can answer that question.

So what we have for openers are the poem and Jawjub:

charge a short hop
pick it, flick it
toward the reaching mitt
the man is out
he's out
sit him down
he can curse
dash his helmet to the ground
moan away to no avail
the soft hand flicker
oh so quick
got him by a hair

Chance Caine wrote that to show how he liked to get 'em—the ones who hit it to short and expect to beat it at first. The quicks, the little lefty speedsters, the punchers, the ones who throw a roostertail behind them as they sprint down the line. He does not like giving up infield hits. "Get your glove ready, Caine." That's what Willie Jawjub said. Willie the Weasel. Chance got him one day four times. Jawjub was a chopper. Put it in play and blaze down the line. He went at Chance four times, and four times Chance got him on the bang-bang at first. Sweet William Jawjub choreographed his spinning leaps of rage at the umpire's calls beautifully. He sure knew how to decorate an out. Jawjub. Sweet William. Of himself, he said, "Singles, slashers, chalk kickers—that was me. Loved to get them infielders running around, falling down, throwing the ball, eating dirt, losing their hats, looking funny. And me standing on second base. Made Chance Caine throw it away twice in one game, and if that's not a record, it should be. Ended up on third both times. I had to dig a little. 'Just hit it to short, podner. Hit it to short. He'll boot it.' And under my breath to myself I say, yeah, hit it to short, he'll boot another one . . . eventually . . . sometime . . . maybe."

I look at life this way. You're dropped from the womb onto your personal conveyer belt to death. Sometimes it's a rough ride. You've got to hang on when it tilts sideways or navigates a bumpy section. You can fall off before you reach the end. Or you can safely complete the whole ride and topple off like in the cartoons, when you reach down, feel nothing under you, realize you're suspended in mid-air, and with that realization, plummet. Some belts are short. Some stretch way off into the creaky distance. Like the one that belonged to 106-year-old San Francisco waiter and former Houdini assistant Larry Lewis. Okay?

CHANCE

Let's say Chance Caine is seventeen, eighteen years on his conveyer belt ride. He's playing in Florida in an Instructional League. The Lion manager, Stony Babcock, drops by to take a look at the rooks. Some years later in a *Sporting News* interview, he says, "When I seen Chance Caine first, he was playing winter ball and Lester Carpens my scout who had signed him was screaming over the phone to me all the time to come and look at this new franchise marvel phenom and I am impressed on account of Lester doesn't go wild hog ever very rarely and is mostly close to the vest serious at all times in fact but I did go round to have a look and if his hands was visible I didn't see it but the play was made at first and I blinked a few times or two and said to Lester I think you got me a ballplayer.

"And I won't say nothing about that man what punched me on the face for no good reason but I wasn't drove out of the big leagues by that and who won the Series between me and the Lions that next year is all I want to know."

There's clarity for you. A picture of Stony Babcock: runty bowlegged body topped with a fat wrinkly white-haired head. Big old hands. Gnarled. That's the word. I like that word.

gnarled

His hands were gnarled. Old catcher's beat-up hands. He's the Lion manager for a chunk of Chance's time. He's the guy who said, "Why not now? If it's not too early, it's not too late." And that said, Chance Caine jumped from Rookie League to Major league starting shortstop.

I'm going to tell you a lot of lies. I told you that before. But I'm telling you again so you'll remember. I don't want to be on the receiving end of the new American dream— a successful lawsuit. When I tell you what happened, maybe it didn't happen. Remember that. I hope they put this on the fiction shelf anyway. We're talking art here. Okay? Non-verbal communication. It's all lies. Or it isn't. Whatever.

There's a guy who wore checkerboard jackets, a bald sportswriter called Ben Blessee, he's part of the story. A blowhard know-it-all glad hand smarmy bastard suck up. He wrote excrement, but he was there at Chance's rookie spring training. He spewed:

CHANCE

THERE IS CREAM IN THIS CROP
by Ben Blessee

The Arizona desert sky is clear and new this spring, and the ballplayers have come back to retune their bodies to play the game of the green diamond. The old-timers, the veterans, move about confidently, relaxed. The young unknowns, eager to impress, race about fiercely, magnifying in their minds a thousandfold the tiny mistakes they make that might send them deep into the minors. There is one who is different. He is an 18-year-old shortstop. His name is Chance Caine.

Yesterday, as I sat behind home plate soaking up sun and surveying the great herd of hopefuls running through drills, Lion superscout Les Carpens walked over and sat down beside me. "Ben, watch the kid on short," he said. I looked out to shortstop and saw one of the youngsters wearing a number in the nineties waiting to field. He is nothing special to look at. He stands 5'10", weighs 175 pounds. He was poised, knees bent, staring in at coach Flappy Byness, who had tossed a ball into the air to swing at with his fungo bat and send a sharp grounder to the waiting fielder. I saw the ball shoot to the boy's right. He had backhanded it and sent it on to first before I could see what had happened. "See that?" said Carpens. I watched this boy field for five minutes as Byness tried in every way to get one through him. He had hands faster than I have ever seen in fifteen years covering the Lions. Everything is possible early in the spring under the Arizona desert sky. Take my advice. Remember one name. Chance Caine.

And so on, blah, blah, blah. But that's enough. There's the scoop. Okay. Blessee's luck. The biggest scoop of his life. Of course, it was Les Carpens who had nudged him in the side and forced him to look out at the field and watch Chance, interrupting Blessee's chatting blather with Everett Mander, owner of the Lions. Old Lester Carpens. He was the one who saw the Chance Caine greatness first. Chance was kind of hard to notice until someone grabbed you, made you look at what he was doing. They always said about him in high school that he got the job done, had a good glove, was a decent hitter. The things the scouts wrote were: average arm, no power, average speed, good hands. Somewhere in the walled turreted Spanish tiled lush gardened compound that is Chance Caine's home, there is a framed piece of paper. It is a scouting report in Les Carpen's careful handwriting. It says: "This boy is average and adequate in all phases of the game. However, if I live long enough, I swear I will see this boy enshrined at Cooperstown as I have never seen quicker hands ever than what this boy has got." Lester Carpens is gone, and he didn't see Chance Caine go into the Hall of Fame. But he stuck around long enough to see Caine phone in his reservation.

Lester Carpens and Ichabod Crane. Twin stick-men. There's the picture. Baseball wasn't around when Ichabod was fleeing the headless horseman, so it's useless to wonder if he could pitch like Lester Carpens. Lester Carpens, 6'5", sidearm sinker. Pitched a no-hitter. 22 ground balls. Discovered Chance Caine.

Kenny Elias, Chance's high school baseball coach, talked into the tape recorder in his living room. He's got a comfortable couch. I ate some of the cookies to be polite. God, they were bad. No sugar. Health food guy. He said:

"When I managed Chance Caine in high school, we didn't have much of a team—just Chance and Bobby Ullett. Most of the scouts were coming around to check out Bobby. He threw lefthanded heat and was a prospect, though he never did sign. And as for Chance, he simply made it look too easy, I guess. He made it look as like he never got a tough bounce. He was always there making the plays. He was my regular shortstop even when he was a somewhat undersized sophomore, probably 5'5", maybe 120 pounds. Picked up all the grounders, looped his throws to first. He went on weights or something after his sophomore year, because he was 30 pounds heavier and 4 inches taller as a junior. His arm wasn't pattycake anymore, but it didn't have major league written on it either. You know why people ignored his hitting? We always saw second line pitching. The scouts would say that. They'd tell me, 'That's a good little shortstop you got.' He was 5'10" and 170 pounds his senior year. Not exactly a midget. At any rate, one day after we'd lost another and I was stashing bats in the bag, I looked out on the field and saw Lion scout Les Carpens standing near the left field line talking with Chance and Chance's mom. Well, you know Chance never looks excited, but there he was, grinning his head off and pumping his right hand, squeeze, squeeze, squeeze. Well, damn, I said to myself, the Lions are going to sign him. Well, that's fine."

Sign him they did. I'm telling you they sent the young man to Idaho. It was rookie time. And the teacher of the rookie Caine was the right person. Another break for Chance. The man was Honey Brown. I talked to him, too. Hey. Watch out. The story's flowing now. Honey Brown said:

"I never did like Stony Babcock much, and I played eight years of shortstop with the Lions for him and Everett Mander. I was there the only world championship they got, if you'll recall. There's a notion that they put me out in Idaho to manage that rookie team because of Chance

Caine. You get the idea. Wanting me to show him the ropes. Wrong. They didn't know Chance Caine from any whoozis. Truth is I asked Mr. Mander for a job managing in the low minors. I wanted to work with the raw new kids. It was spring training time. My legs were through, and I didn't feel like being taped from thigh to ankle every day. So Mr. Mander accepted my retirement and gave me that manager job all in the space of fifteen minutes in his office."

A Diary Journal Notebook With Shiny Green Cover

It's chock full o' goodies. Chance carried it with him and wrote in it all during his fatefilled final and 22nd season with the Lions. That last season. We'll spend a lot of time there. But the shiny green diary's first entry is:

> My first professional manager was Honey Brown, the old shortstop. Old? He was four years younger than I am now when he managed me in my one minor league season. At that time, I thought he was older than God. I guess that makes me four years older than guys older than God.

That's not one of my lies. When I quote from the diary, I won't be lying too often. Sometimes I'll even give you a lie alert. Other times, too bad. I'm warning you now. Get ready for the Idaho teammate's memory trip.

Robby Brightbox speaks:

"There aren't many guys out there who can say that they played minor league ball with Chance Caine. I'm one of them. And I'll tell you what it was like. A great clubhouse we had. Smell of piss, piss stains, piss-yellow paint on the walls. Concrete floor. Your locker? A hook that tilted down and dropped your shirt off as soon as you hung it on. The fans? Old, old, old, OLD guys, assorted drunks you couldn't tell the sex of, teenagers doing drugs and humping in the far right field and left field corners of the stands, a psychotic who walked back and forth behind home plate droning 'get a hit, get a hit, get a hit, get a hit' all during the game non-stop no matter which team was batting and even between innings when nobody was batting, a fat lady with no teeth who sat behind our dugout, laughing like a horse punched in the neck, and occasionally leaning over to say, 'I'm with ya, I'm with ya, we gottem.'

"Honey Brown was the manager. Couldn't understand a word the man said. His mouth was always full of tobacco and he had these little brown rivers of juice running out the corners. When he spit, it was like somebody threw a gallon bucket of slop against a wall. He managed to teach us some baseball using a wigwag system and grunts. 'Haybah, haybah!' was what he yelled at us when anything went right. It was only two weeks into the season and we were calling Chance 'Haybah.'

"Well, we had Ladies Night, we had Old Timers Night, we had Knight Day (pre-game joust!), we had Farmer Day, Chocolate Bar Day, Ostrich Day. I won the ostrich race, fell off the damn thing and it kicked me. Here I am a young man aiming to be the major league home run king, and I'm riding ostriches in Idaho. But the thing was, I had some power and could play a decent first base. Called myself Saver of Bad Throws. Mister Scoop. Mister Dancer of the Toe Around the Bag. Chance Caine in the field was a bore to me. Never had to save a bad throw because he never made one. Go to the bag. Stick out your mitt. The ball is there in the chest every time. Ho hum. I had style. He had talent.

"Boy, it was something. I loved it. From that team only Chance Caine made it to what they call 'the show' now. There's two dozen guys scattered all over the country getting old together and telling anybody who will listen about how they played ball with Chance Caine in the Idaho Rookie League. Myself, I'd go back in a second.

Trade in Brightbox Trucking, my pool and sauna for one more summer riding around in a bus with a bunch of guys, playing baseball in empty wooden ballparks, eating bad and sleeping rarely. In other words, I wish I was young. But it ended for me when I was twenty-four. On the day I quit I said, 'I'll buy me a truck, god damn it.' I only made it to Double A. I wasn't going to get any further. So I decided to ship furniture instead. I've got no regrets. I had my fun. I gave it my full shot. Came up not good enough. That's the story."

I read that Brightbox stuff to Honey Brown. He explained to me, with impeccable diction, how he had to give up the tobacco because too many lumpy things started growing in his mouth. I also got from him:

"The transition from being a player to being a manager wasn't tough for me. I was twice as old as my players, and I was only thirty-six. I was a young man, but I thought I was old. Say, give me another shot at thirty-six again and I'll be nothing but happy. Hell, I'll even take forty-six. Now about Chance Caine. I'm not going to bullshit you. The first time I watched him field I got the goosebumps. Yes, sir. I am a shortstop. I know what is going on. I had just finished up a twelve-year major league career playing shortstop. There I was in Idaho running a bunch of fuzzfaces through drills to see what I had, and one of the fuzzfaces was better right then than I had ever been! 'Protect that gold' was the first thought in my head. 'Protect that gold.'"

The gold was protected. The gold married the high school sweetheart, name of Alice Rowe, after winning unanimous Rookie of the Year and the first of twenty-two consecutive Gold Gloves for the gold's fielding prowess. The gold theme. The golden touch. In the world of baseball, he had it. The rookie year: .314 batting average, 44 doubles, 6 triples, 5 home runs, 103 runs scored, 79 driven in. Outside the baseball world . . . well. Alice Rowe, after Chance signed his multi-year, multimillion-dollar contract, joined him on an eighteen year voyage through an empty marriage. What can I tell you about Alice Rowe Caine? I've got scanty data on her. That's the way she wants it. I explained to her this project that I was taking on, and in her deep strong smooth voice she said, "I am unimpressed by all the hoopla and don't wish to be bothered by it. I will say only this. I married too young for improper reasons the wrong person. It was not his fault." That was it. I'm on the phone with her for less than two minutes. I've got her mother's number. I try it.

Marsha King Rowe doesn't want to talk either, says only, "I knew nothing would come to any good." I go through a list of Chance/Alice high school classmates and finally get to Nella Vade. She speaks on the subject of Chance and Alice. Like this:

"Alice Caine has had a tough time. It's hard for her to be happy, with her mother and all. In high school she was aloof and quiet. We all thought she was stuck up. We couldn't figure out how she latched onto Chance. Everybody would have died to go out with Chance. That includes me. I was no exception. My dad was the basketball coach, and I tried to use him a few times to lure Chance to the house, but alas, I failed. Well, it's a lot of years from back then to up to now, and everybody from our group has had a lot of life lived. I've had a few swell surprises in life, I can tell you. Maybe now I'm a wise old lady. Well, not real old, not yet. But old enough to have learned a few things. Do I know some things about Chance and Alice? Yes, but I'm not talking. That's one of the things I've learned. To keep my trap shut."

Nella Vade's keeping her trap shut. Should I? Of course not. You've got to know the dirt . . . if there is any.

Supermarket trash tabloid world lives. Stay tuned for the UFOs and the gunplay—this is not a lie. But for now, let's head back to baseball. This chapter's been plenty long enough.

② Monkey Joe

I want to describe what I look like so you'll know who's talking to you better. My twin flickers at you from the silent comedies and later from the soundies with Stan and Ollie. Do you know Jimmy Finlayson, bald, walrus mustached, short, master of the squinty eye take? Picture him without a pie in his face and you've got me—shy smile, digging with my index finger at my dimple, if I had one. Okay?

As for Chance Caine, well, the baseball world turned around and there he was, in place and playing, as if he had always been there, as if he would always be there, the eternal shortstop, perfect, out of nowhere, dropped into the position with a neatness like my neighbor's lawn, which looks tucked in at the corners. There's a sentence. Wow. I either apologize for or am proud of the tucked in lawn bit. I can't decide yet. More to the point, I have Chance's green diary in front of me, and I'm looking for a story he told me he had written in it. It has to do with fear and a wild fast pitcher. If I turn to the right page, I'll see:

Once, and only once, I was scared on the baseball field. It was on a day when I had to bat against Monkey Joe Huddleston. He was a player who, like me, had a gift born in him. His arms were long whips. His hands seemed to hang below his knees. Thus the nickname. He had a fastball that cut the air at 100 mph plus. The unfortunate thing for him and for all who batted against him was that Monkey Joe had only the faintest notion where the ball was going once it left his hand.

I was 18 years old. I had completed my first pro season in Idaho and was playing in the Florida Winter Instructional League. Monkey Joe was there, too, seven years in the minors behind him, still searching for the miracle of control. The Lion pitching coach then was old Nelson Pick. He was out there daily working on Monkey's mechanics. I could hear his nonstop pep talk while I was out there eating up the ground balls Flappy Byness had me chasing. Nelson was saying things like, 'Concentration, Monk, concentration. In your mind. In your mind. Focus in. Focus. Slow, slow, slow. Reach and follow. Plant, whip, follow, head up. Hot damn! That's it. Explosion. Good one, good one. You're right there, pal. You got the release point. You got it.' Monkey Joe answered with little grunts, 'Yeh, yeh.'

So one day we come out to play and they've got Monkey Joe Huddleston warming up on the mound. He's going to pitch AGAINST us. He's ready to try Nelson Pick's theories and a new-found confidence. I'm watching very carefully. I know all about Monkey Joe, and a feeling I've not known before begins to happen in my stomach as Monkey's first warmup pitch hisses loudly high above and beyond the catcher and smashes into the backstop. I am to be the leadoff hitter. Monkey looks to Nelson. Nelson gives him a shaky thumbs up. Monkey nods. The catcher handles three of the next five, gives me a you-poor-dumb-bastard look and adjusts the multiple sponge arrangement he has in his mitt. Then Monkey waves his hand that he's ready. I want to wave mine that I'm not, but I am so young that I take a deep breath and step into the batter's box. I look out to the mound. The man is one very long arm with a huge hand gripping the ball in a white-knuckled clench. In his eyes I see great fear. Seeing his fear, my fear triples. No windup, small leg kick, and here comes that long whip over the top whipping and Monkey grunts in effort and the ball skips on a hard rise through the air and bends the catcher's glove back into his chest for strike one. My fear subsides. My hands are quick. I could have put the bat on that. I'm ready to hit now. The second pitch is four feet behind me. Fear returns, never more to roam. I am now playing dodge ball. I am no longer a hitter. The next one hits eight feet in front of the plate, leaps up and shatters a bar in the catcher's mask. 'Concentration, focus, you got it,' the high whine of Nelson Pick. Monkey Joe nodding.

Catcher comes back with new head gear. From my position huddled in the deepest reaches of the batter's box, I agree with the umpire on strike two. Ball three is a relief because it's six feet outside. I hear somebody yell, 'Good eye.' Funny now. Not funny then. I looked at Monkey Joe and could see him straining to concentrate, straining to focus, straining to know he got it, and on his face I knew he knew he didn't got it and never would. Ball four almost killed me. I think of my quickness as a sort of mutation, a gift from God, and it saved my life right there with that ball coming directly at my head 100 mph plus. I quicked my head straight back. The ball said sssshhhh as it brushed my lips going by. A kiss of death. The genuine article.

Nice story. Nice story. I like the story. There are good stories everywhere. Here's a true story that will get you. Watch this. I myself personally once knew a woman who broke her nose flushing her toilet. Okay? That is the fact known. Nose broken flushing toilet. Make up your own how-it-happened. I have knowledge of the true how-it-happened and it is pretty good. Why don't you let your cranial neurons dance a while? Sorry. It's the instructor in me. You figure it out.

I've got something for you from the other side of the Caine and the wild man confrontation. I found the guy. The Monkey Joe Huddleston. I'll tell you something. To shake hands with the man is to lose sight and to lose communication with your right arm from slender wrist to where you suppose your fingertips quiver deep in the flesh cavern of Joe Huddleston's hand. He gave a speech into my tape recorder. He said:

"My name is Joseph Huddleston, and I am an alcoholic. I have not had a drink in seventeen years. Though I was unaware of it at the time, one of the most significant days in my entire life was the day my arm exploded on me and I was finally able to stop trying to become some big time top pitcher. I was given the arm, but I wasn't given the mastery of it. Nope. In fact, my friend, it was the other way around. Back then I asked myself one thousand times if I asked myself one time why did I have this arm? What was it for? My ball was timed at 112 miles per hour. What good is that? My arm gave out and I fell to sinning for three years after—drinking, feeling sorry for myself. Let me tell you, I was a great celebrity bum around here moaning to everybody about how rotten my luck was that my arm went out on me just after I had found the secret of control. The secret of control! Hog-wash! Absolutely. I never found the secret. But that became my new excuse to drink. My old excuse about having no control had become obsolete. Had outlived its usefulness, like me. Yes, I was miserable.

"But, praise God, I found the Lord, working through my wonderful wife, Penny. She helped me to rise from the muck and to realize that I was a child of God and to accept our Savior into my heart. I know now that my arm was Satan's gift that led me into temptation for personal glory and riches. I now use my pitching hand to reach out to my fellow man in friendship and for the glory of God. I'm on the Lord's team now. I'm pitching joy and salvation. Bless you, sir."

Okay, Monkey Joe. Okay, big fella. You were the only man on a ball field to ever endanger the cleanliness of Chance Caine's underwear. I'd say that's something. Isn't it?

I like short chapters. This one is over after the following short poem.

> lad
> step into the big leagues
> you have survived
> minor league pitchers
> with major league arms
> and absolutely
> no control

3

Rainbow

Between ultraviolet and infrared, the ribbon's long curve arches in the sky, solid and strong. Then it disappears. What do you know about Clara Bow? Was Mary Pickford an ancient recluse hidden in her castle at the end? Who was Mary Pickford anyhoo? Some of you say that. Right? Okay. That's what I'm talking about sometimes. The Andy Warhol thing. Has the spotlight been on you for fifteen minutes yet? You say who is Andy Warhol? I say forget it. I say, "And now, back to our story."

Let me put down here the managers' thoughts on

Chance Caine. Big wrinkle head, Stony Babcock, and the man with the permanent wide-eyed surprise look, Flappy Byness. When asked to list his best defense, Stony started:

"Well, if you're going to talk about gloves, there's no two ways. You've got to take a Chance, just got to, as there is no other delicacy to stand up there with him in either department. Firstly, secondly, thirdly, it's all in a day's work, and you know how the manager loves to accumulate outs in easy packages on the defense. There's Caine. And that's it.

The only other shortstop I ever had on my side who was close to Chance wasn't even close. And that was that redhead who liked the ladies more than enough and helped make me wrinkly."

And Flappy Byness, in response to a similar question, spooned out, "When I put a ball club out on the field, I want those young men to play baseball. I want my team to get those outs on defense and to make those hits on offense. We need to put some numbers up on the scoreboard if we're going to win the ball game. There's only one way to do something in baseball. And that's to do it. Chance Caine is the finest fielder who ever picked up a ground ball and then threw the ball to first base. I make no exceptions. This is a man who knows with completeness what to do with a baseball, be it with the glove or with the bat. This man wears his uniform when he plays the game. I am proud to be privileged to pencil his name in on my lineup card each day we play."

Meanwhile, back at Babcock, Stony babbled on, "And for what other reason than that did we reassemble our farms to manufacture sinker balls? What's the use if it's in the air and your shortstop can't get it? We want nice easy ground balls or even nasty ones. It don't make a difference. They're outs and they know it."

Are there really guys who talk like that? You'd be surprised.

What if I told you there was a pitcher with the Lions named Rainbow Clouds? What if I told you he might say, "The Rainbow reigned supreme. He could plant his seed where he would, make it sing for sixty feet six inches and all in the fractional twinkling of an eye."? I could say, for instance, that he was born Jesse Cornell. That he changed his name to Rainbow Clouds when he stormed into the majors with a 14 strikeout one-hitter. That his comet lasted for ten years and 253 wins before he blew his arm away and went off with his family. Let's say he bought an island somewhere warm. Chance Caine has been there. Rainbow has said, "Come over for good, Mister Sixes. We can build a house for you down the other side of the bay." Did I tell you about Mister Sixes? It's a Chance nickname. He wore number 66 on his uniform. But you probably knew that. Let's pretend all this Rainbow stuff I just told you is true. So Chance says,

> A pair of genetic freaks disguised as normal human beings—Rainbow and me. God said about me, 'Give him the quickest reactions of any man, two times faster than he who is second.' Of Jesse, I mean Rainbow, He said, 'Make his arm long and whippy with giant hands and long slender fingers so that he might make that curve ball spin, and in addition, give him the gift of complete accuracy and command of all his pitches. Furthermore, let him be the lousiest of hitters.'

Ho ho. Chance make a joke.

Here is the place right here where we want to try to answer the following question. How did Stony Babcock enjoy having a flamboyant Hall of Fame pitcher on his staff? His answer, "There are some guts out there that I love and some guts out there that I hate." For a deeper analysis, I now call on Carl "Father" Frisch, former relief pitcher and well known thinker of thoughts, much like the Scarecrow of Oz. He was an eyewitness to the Stony-Rainbow main event. He's going to tell you:

"Hey, you know, I'm only a rookie when this thing happens, but I got a theory about the Stony-Rainbow thing. Well, you know, it's not even a theory it's so damn obvious. A lot of people call Stony Babcock a racist. Way off. Forget it. You know? That's not the thing we're talking about here. What it was was this. It was that the Rainbow got too much ink, too much media, too much limelight. Get it? Too many newsers stood around his locker after the game, not enough coming to hear Stony perform, you know. Hey, simple enough. Stony hates loud superstars. They crowd his space. Right?"

Right. That's why. But what? What happened? What was the deal? I'm going to tell you. One night I gave an assignment to the class in which Chance was a student. I told them to write about a confrontation or conflict that they had observed or been part of in their own lives. He turned in this:

On the day I'm talking about, the Rainbow got buried in a squall of basehits. It was during the time I spent a couple of weeks out of the lineup with a mangled up hamstring. I could look over at Stony's face from my perch at the end of the bench. Yes. Hatred was there, and a grim little smile. And his gaze was settled out there on that little hill in the middle of the diamond, watching Rainbow take his lumps. Six straight hits. Rainbow mopping his brow. Connell came out to the mound from behind the plate, stared into the dugout at Stony. Stony was a statue, grim little smile. Made no move. Somebody lined out. Then two more hits. The Rainbow had had it. He removed himself from the game, walked into the dugout silence, went up to Stony and laid him out on the floor with a short powerful punch to the jaw delivered with his precious left hand. He then walked down the runway to the clubhouse without looking back. Well, the upshot was that Rainbow told his press conference that the bossman would have to choose between Clouds and the manager. Stony made a similar statement, only it took him a half hour longer. He was confident that Everett

Mander would back him for the good of the team. Fat chance, Stony. I said that in my mind from where I sat in front of my locker stripping down to get some treatment for my leg. Reporters asked me what I thought. I stared them away and limped into the training room, closing the racket off behind me. 'Hop right in, Chance,' said Billy, our trainer. 'Got any ideas about who the new manager's gonna be?' 'Don't care,' said I. Stony got the axe the next day. And they gave the job to Flappy Byness. Flappy, the Clown.

There you are. That's what happened. An efficient felling of a Babcock. A one punch knockout. I went to Mander Stadium to collect some interviews and looked at the mound from which Rainbow descended to deliver his fistal message to Stony. I was waiting in the first row of boxes behind third base for Tim Connell, Rainbow's catcher on that day and on all other days, for that matter. He's the Lion pitching coach now. He has grown enough sideways since his playing days ended so that he's now almost as wide as he is tall. They call him 'Round.' He spoke to me:

"If this is going to be written down, I want to say it right. I'm a catcher. I caught in the National League for 12 years, all with the Lions. Now I am their pitching coach. Do you have that? Okay. The single most standing out thing about those Lion teams I was on, for me, was Rainbow Clouds. If you want to ask me what I want to have carved on my tombstone, I'll tell you.

TIM CONNELL
RAINBOW CLOUDS' CATCHER

"When I came up to the Lions I could hit a little. I hung around the .260 mark for my first four years. Then the nicks and bangs of the catching day in, day out began to knock points off the average. But I could still catch, and anyway they didn't need hitting from me with our lineup. I caught Rainbow his whole career, and he was the only pitcher I was catching my last three years. I was his designated catcher. We were tuned in. He never shook my sign off, because I always called exactly what he wanted. The only way you ever saw me on the cover of a magazine was standing next to Rainbow. And those were because he told them, 'Get one of the battery. The battery has two terminals. Get us together.' Our last year he won his 20th on the last day of the season. In the clubhouse he came over to me before the reporters got there and said, 'Battery, my arm hurts. It is time to fade away.' We were tuned in, like I said. I knew he was telling me I'd played my last game, too. He was right. I stood with him when he told the group of reporters. He said, 'People, the battery is dead. Cannot be recharged another time. Clouds and Connell bid you farewell.' I remember every word exactly, just like it was. I've been on his island. The wife and kids have spent whole summers there. Now you're not going to ask me about Stony Babcock, are you? Pig-eyed runt son of a bitch. That's my Stony Babcock statement."

I almost asked him if he could expand on that Babcock statement, but I decided against it. Instead, I thanked him for his time and as he rolled away down to the bullpen to mentor his flingers, I thought about Rainbow Clouds borrowing a bit of General Doug's line about old soldiers not dying, but just fading away. Then I looked out over to where Chance Caine had stood his ground for 22 seasons, making plays that made press box denizens stand up off their fat sarcastic asses. There were a couple of guys playing pepper in front of the NO PEPPER sign, tossing the ball between their legs or behind their backs to the batter punching little one-hoppers back at them. Again I looked to the mound where Rainbow Clouds had ruled and imagined the path to the dugout he had taken to deck Stony Babcock. Stuff happened here. People wrote about it. People remember it. Rainbow's 31 win, 4 loss season after Flappy Byness became manager. They remember the Lions winning the division, then falling behind 3 games to 1 in the National League Championship Series against the Pirates. Flappy, wide-eyed surprised, summed up his team's position, "We don't need a three-game winning streak. What we need is a one-game winning streak three times in a row." Going around to the basement and coming up through the back door, that makes sense. Flappy got two of the one-game streaks he needed, but couldn't manage to produce the third one. He would have to wait another full year to get his first crack at managing in the Fall Classic, the World Series. But meanwhile, over there in the American League, Red Pugh had slumped badly, finishing with a .243 batting average and a paltry, for him, 22 home runs. He wondered if he was washed up at 29, and he wondered how it would be to play for Stony Babcock, who would be Detroit's new manager the following year. How was he to know that the stage was being set for his name to live forever in the annals of his sport? They didn't have the Psychic Hotline in those days.

MENTAL EXERCISE FOR CHAPTER 3

How many lies did I tell you? And why? Discuss. Feel free to cheat.

I'm adding an appendix to this chapter. It isn't a small, saclike appendage of the large intestine. It is additional or supplementary material.

A SHORT LIST OF NON-OBSCENE INSULTS

1. You been dominated, suckface.
2. In your dreams, honeyfish.
3. History to you, baby.
4. You small, saclike appendage of a large intestine.

4

Copter

Callas Onassis Jackie JFK Joe Kennedy Gloria Swanson Keystone Kop Fatty Arbuckle Chaplin Oona Eugene O'Neill Ah Wilderness Geraldine Nashville and so on forever Country music Grand Ol Opry Roy Acuff Amen. I call it the linklink game. I play it in my mind a lot. Do you fear for my sanity? Fear not and read this, the mental illness chapter.

Lou Copter. Another name. I know. I move too fast. Everybody tells me that. Sorry. That's the way it is. That's the way it happens. Be patient. It all falls together neatly later. Okay? Let me try to help you with the cast so far. Try to remember these names:

Chance Caine, the main guy
Stony Babcock, his first Lion manager
Flappy Byness, his other Lion manager
Ben Blessee, the sportswriter
Alice, the wife
Rainbow Clouds, the pitcher
Carl 'Father' Frisch, relief pitcher philosopher

These people will be back a lot of times before I have finished doing whatever it is that I am doing. There are others I haven't told you about yet, including the number one most important other than Chance Caine person that there is in this story. And I don't think it's Lou Copter, or 'Lulu' Copter, as they called him at the beginning. I could be lying and not even know it, though.

Copter was the new young hero unveiled by the Lions early in the spring training session of Chance's sophomore season. A fleet base-stealing center fielder, he posed with Chance for a *Sports Illustrated* cover story which asked, 'Will Lions Boast Back-to-Back Rookies of the Year?' Copter answered the question in the affirmative with 83 stolen bases and a .287 batting average. The following year halfway through the season he was dragged in rigid catatonia from the Lion clubhouse, was institutionalized for a few years, then released due to lack of funds for his care. He's one of the homeless, street-dwelling mentally ill. What happened? I'm digging into Chance's green diary again to start. It says:

Sometimes I wonder about Lou Copter. Whatever became of him? Something sure ate him up. He was so skittish, jumpy, nervous, fast talking. If he got picked off first it was like he had a heart attack. He'd be trembling all over. And mumbling while he shook his head 'I'm sorry I'm sorry I'm sorry I'm sorry' like that over and over. And he couldn't be soothed with a 'Don't worry, it happens' or a 'Get him next time.' For a year and a half he fought himself hard, then he unravelled completely almost in a second. I watched it happen right in front of my eyes. He had singled and was taking his lead, trying to get into scoring position so I could drive him in. He got caught leaning the wrong way and was picked off. His late dive back to first left him spread out with his face in the dirt. He didn't move. I thought he was hurt. But then he got very slowly to his feet and walked even more slowly toward the dugout. I was handing my bat to the batboy and getting my glove in return since the pickoff had been the third out. The rest of the guys were jogging out to their defensive positions, but I watched Copter heading for the bench. Hen Philpott tossed Copter's glove at him and moved out to the field. But Lou ignored the glove as it bounced off his leg to the ground. He walked like a zombie into the dugout and up the runway to the clubhouse. Stony yelled something at him and Flappy got up and followed Copter. In a minute, Aaron Hollis came out and took Copter's spot in center, and the game continued. We got them out fast, and when we came in, Stony said something like 'The kid is in some need of guts.' I was up first and grounded out. I ran back into the clubhouse and saw Lou Copter there folded up stiff under a bench. Flappy was there. 'I called Mr. Mander,' he said. 'We're getting the ambulance. Go back and play the game, Chance. I'll take care of this young man.' Copter was gone. Nuts. Psycho. They put him away. For good, I suppose. He was the number one hot topic for a while. Then not. Maybe he's okay now and out. I wonder.

Chance wondered if Copter was out. Oh, he's out. Yes, he's out. Is he okay? On some planets his behavior would probably be considered normal. But not on this one. Afraid not. A ragged coat and a black wool watch cap which might possibly have been another color long ago were what Copter wore when he talked into my tape recorder under a bridge over a stink creek in a San Francisco suburb. Why did he talk to me? How did I find him? I don't think he talked to me. He was barely aware that I was there. Maybe it wasn't him. But it was. He has a sister. She knew where he was. There was some sort of communication from me to him. Something I said slid through. I don't know what it was, but it got him going. He went:

"Smoke is damaging me. That's why it is very important for me to make preparations. There's nothing wrong with baseball. It's such a trivial speck in the universe. If there is infinity, I will be back again and again the same. I'll be you, too. It's not important, but it is noteworthy. Worth noting. Write that. Try to keep your distance. It's not right for you to get that close. There are too many things that have happened to me, but their importance is minimal. It doesn't matter at all. Meaningless. I have collected some very important material, but I'm not going to show it to you. Why should I? Are you important? You aren't important. Not enough. WHY ARE YOU ASKING ME ABOUT THAT GAME!!?? It's all right. It doesn't matter. It's not important. If there is a problem, I'll tell it to you. The problem is the uniform. That's the problem. I don't know. I don't know. HOW THE HELL ARE YOU SUPPOSED TO KEEP A WHITE UNIFORM CLEAN!!?? They never asked me. Does it matter? Not at all. I can tell you about that game. It's stupid. It makes me vomit. It stinks. But it does not matter. It's totally unimportant. Go ahead, throw the damn ball. What do I care? Anybody who plays the game is so stupid. Little damn ball. Throw it over there. Run after it over here. Pick it up. Put it down. Stick it up your ass! Who cares? I've got some important things with me. There's too much smoke in the world. Can you see me? Write about the smoke. Write an article. It might be important. Buy me something."

He wanted SuzyQs. So I bought him six packages of them. He was hugging them to his chest and peering furtively around when I left. I went home.

I called Carl Frisch and talked to him about Copter. I counted on 'Father' Frisch to come up with theories about the hows and the whys of things. On this occasion, he opined: "I got a theory. It's about what it takes to be rich. You know. The thing is, to be rich you've got to be crazy, you know, a real fanatic. You've got to do something that brings the money rolling into your face. Like be a fanatical something. Or be lucky enough to be born in a family where an ancestral nut made the dough, you know? Of course, you're probably a nut there anyway, too, being the genetic descendant of a nut. Like Krupps. You know, the iron works German family. The first Krupp, the guy who built it up, he had his office over the stables because he liked the smell of shit wafting up through the floor! I rest my case. I heard some stories about Mr. Everett Mander's gramps, too, and how he got the money to buy the Lions. Everett himself isn't exactly Ned Normal, you know. An odd person. So are we all. So are we all. Right? Take Chance Caine. There was one genuine A number one phenomenal rich fanatic. Drove himself to perfect his perfection. Had to take so many million grounders every day, you know, every single day! If practice made perfect, he went beyond deity. What a loon. Rich though. I myself am not a poor person. So I've put in my hours. I'm about as batty as they come on the rung several below Copter. A fanatic? Well, I've got a theory about fanatics. They get rich or they wander around city parks in tattered clothes and wild hair and sleep in doorways. Right?"

Right. They eat a lot of SuzyQs, too. Lou Copter dealt with the pressure of performing on a major league level by going crazy and never coming back. Chance dealt with the pressure by not realizing there was any. You have to know there's pressure for there to be pressure. Wait a minute. I buy my clothes at the thrift store and what hair I have is what you might call wild. However, I delight in my strangeness with a wide toothy grin. Ha ha. Deelighted! Bully! A Teddy Roosevelt moment. Excuse me. What I should be saying is: Was Chance Caine a sober workaholic? Well, maybe not. The Lion mascot, The Lion, has a story to tell:

"I used Chance Caine a lot. He was perfect for me. The dignified superstar. He had all these little mannerisms that were easy to imitate, exaggerate. He didn't care, either. He went right along with it. Like one of my bits was I'm right behind him mirroring everything he's doing between innings. He's taking the practice grounders from first base, and I'm right behind shadowing him with this four-foot-long puffy glove I've got. One day he lets one go through his legs. It bounces off my puff. I pick it up, throw it to first. Chance comes over and mimes that he wants to trade gloves. We trade. He takes a few grounders with the puff. The fans are going nuts. Chance shakes his head no and asks for his glove back. I run out into left with his glove, and he chases me! When he catches me, I get down on my knees and beg for mercy. He pats my head, turns to walk away with my glove. I sneak up and kick him in the ass. The crowd is out of its head. Some of the players hate like hell the clowning I do with the game. I went up to Chance after that time and thanked him for the bit. He said, 'It's a game. Games are supposed to be fun.' Some guys make my job real easy."

This is the insanity chapter. How many of the people we have met in this chapter have displayed unbalanced minds? What percentage of anything anybody said is cacophonously senseless drivel!? What are we learning about Chance Caine? Anything yet? Try the following. I told Chance's class to write a science fiction or fantasy story. Chance Caine turned in

GÖTTERDÄMMERUNG
by Chance Caine

WHEN THE WORLD COLLAPSED IT WAS HELLO, MY FRIEND, YOU YELLOW BRICK ROAD.

We all know now what we didn't know then. Despite the wearing of cowboy hats in board-rooms of giant corporations, an inevitably laugh-able game was played out to its too obvious conclusion. Old wounds were opened, examined, and closed. Whale language was learned, and what they said was, "Don't save us."

THE SPACE VOYAGE IS IN PROGRESS.

A better mouse trap had been invented. Snow shoes worked. But what a useless travesty. All that glittered soon lay crushed and broken on the sands of indecision. And nowhere was this felt more than over there, just behind that little hillock.

THE UNIVERSE IS LARGE.

Clues were abundant and lay undigested deep in the laminated maw of time. And yet, in the all-inclusive desperation of hope, a new mood was born—a flinty resolution, a plucky stoicism, a new found hardness, a kind of spiky intelligence, horned. Nevertheless, the world ended.

WE CAN'T GO HOME AGAIN.

Some surviving optimists strolled about giving comfort to the sorrowing. "Look here," reasoned one, "let's say God had a choice to make: the destruction of the world on the one hand, or the release on compact disc of 'The Chipmunks Sing Gershwin' on the other. We can only give thanks that He made the right choice."

IT WAS NEVER LIKE THIS IN THE MOVIES.

Some died with their boots on. Others died never having owned a pair of boots. One absolutely famous ballerina known the world over by name died with her toe shoes on. The entire New York Philharmonic died, instruments to lips. 'Kiss My Violin', a major new work by an anonymous composer, was in the last throes of the first movement when the world punched out on that big time clock in the sky.

WE ARGUE ABOUT THE 'BIG BANG.'

The largest buildings remained, but with corners rounded and edges beveled.

THERE IS A RUMOR THAT REALITY IS A MYTH.

Yet who could drown the dream? Only the memory of a certain young man, a peculiar young man, a very strange young man with a certain sort of smile—a smile of sharpened teeth dripping from sharpened gums. Yes, Thomas Jefferson.

WE BEGIN TO EMERGE FROM THE LONG DEPRESSION.

Truth and Beauty reconciled at the very end, though Beauty got in one last little dig.

WE ARE PRODUCING SPACE CHILDREN.

And when one gets right down to it, who was to blame? And why? What for? How come? Huh? Was it merely another one of God's little jokes? Like the poopoo cushion? Or not.

SOME PLANETS ARE ALMOST GOOD ENOUGH FOR US.

Sweet sad memories of things lost crowd upon us, the orphans. The cry of the loon next door. His wife. The touch of cold marble to a trembling buttock. Petrochemicals, effluvia, loam. But mostly I grieve for the flowers and trees. Sad for them to burn never knowing or even suspecting much of anything at all.

WE AREN'T GOOD ENOUGH FOR SOME PLANETS.

In the flashing of an eyelash, it was curtains. Most of the rich lost serious amounts of money. Only those with lead underwear and stock in Orion futures emerged relatively unscathed. However, they too suffered the loss of their lives. The rest of us searched for help.

WHAT WOULD AL EINSTEIN THINK OF ALL THIS?

In the beginning, after the end, when the fourth dimension was made known to us. the lords of the fourth dimension were more than kind. The lords of the fourth dimension were more than patient with us. They were more than protective of us. They were, in fact, drunk. Consequently, we were forced to turn aside from them and to struggle along on our own.

A SHIMMERING BLUE BALL IN SPACE BECKONS.

The human race began when some poor proto-hominid jerk limped home and whined the australopithecine equivalent of "I lost my keys." And though we, that creature's direct descendants, have lost all, all is not lost.

STOUT HEARTS ARISE! NOW IS THE TIME TO UNCLOUD THE WEBS OF YOUR IMAGINATION AND FOLD

UNTO YOUR BOSOM THE BANNER OF A NEW GERM. A
GERM OF AN IDEA OF SUCCESS IN A NEW AND HOSTILE
ENVIRONMENT. AFTER ALL, THE LANDINGS ON THE
MOON OF A PLANET CIRCLING A STAR DISTANT HAVE
GONE PERFECTLY, EXCEPT FOR THOSE MANY SHIPS
WHICH CRASHED AND BURNED. THE PEOPLE ARE CALM,
AND THE FUTURE WILL BE. NOT CALM—BUT OUT THERE
HIDING.

Yes, yes, a thousand times yes! But no.

Now maybe you understand better why I, an old weird
non-athletic poet, am writing a book about a baseball
player. I'm not a fan. I don't care about the records. Even
the infamous Chance Caine Day incident didn't tell me to
write a book. What told me to write the book was a
question that formed in my skull after I read things
Chance Caine wrote. Who is this guy?

Is it time now to go back into the private life? Dig for
the dirt? Find out if he has a favorite color toilet paper?
Stay tuned. I'll start dealing out the personal stuff in the
back half of the next chapter. Scout's honor. Would I lie?

(5)

Building Legends

Lions	AB	R	H	BI	Braves	AB	R	H	BI
Kreen cf	2	3	1	0	Bliss cf	2	0	0	0
Haynes cf	2	0	1	0	Hockney cf	2	0	0	0
Caine ss	4	3	4	3	Mendez 3b	4	1	1	1
Tykus ss	0	0	0	0	Villa 1b	3	0	1	0
Daedalus 1b	5	1	1	2	Kessle lf	3	0	0	0
Pinney rf	5	1	2	3	Barker rf	3	0	0	0
Harris lf	3	0	1	1	Smith c	3	0	0	0
O'Brien	2	0	0	0	Colorado ss	3	0	0	0
Philpott 2b	3	0	2	0	Floater 2b	3	0	0	0
Fanshaw 3b	1	1	0	0	Weeks p	0	0	0	0
Escamillo 3b	2	0	0	0	Olsen ph	1	0	0	0
Connell c	5	1	2	0	Narvin p	0	0	0	0
Clouds p	5	0	0	0	Champolini p	0	0	0	0
	39	10	14	9	Pepper ph	1	0	0	0
					Peron p	0	0	0	0
					Aguaro ph	1	0	0	0
						29	1	2	1

Lions	330 130 000 — 10 14 0
Braves	000 100 000 — 1 2 1

E—Narvin   2B—Caine, Pinney, Philpott   3B —Caine   HR—Caine (14), Pinney (35), Mendez (18).   SB—Haynes (4).   SF—Harris

Lions	IP	H	R	ER	BB	SO
Clouds (W, 25-9)	9	2	1	1	0	5
Braves						
Weeks (L, 14-15)	3	7	6	6	3	1
Narvin	1 1/3	3	4	4	2	0
Champolini	1 2/3	1	0	0	2	3
Peron	3	3	0	0	3	3

T—3:22   A—50,893

That's the box score of one of the games that built the myth that Chance was. I'll tell you it was the last game of the season. I'll tell you that Chance needed to get two hits to nudge his average up and over the .400 mark. Now I'll tell you that there is a big booming bull of a man who was the plate umpire on that day. I held the phone two feet from my ear as he described the game. Umpire Bill (to his friends Un) Able let fly:

"Shit, I was behind the plate the day he hit .400. He needs two for two and he's got it. First time up, that son of a bitch bastard Riley Weeks pitching for the Braves throws the first one right at Caine's head. Shit of a thousand asses, I'm pissed right away and out there warning Weeks that he's outta here if he keeps that shit up. Meanwhile, Caine's just sitting there in the batter's box smiling. He's goddam amused! I get the game going again and Caine takes the next pitch and gently places it into left for a hit. Next time up, before he pulls a double down the right field line, he fouls one back that catches me crash in the face mask and I'm still listening to the chimes as he slides into second. Shit. He's through. He's got .400. The Lions are ahead 6-0 in a nothing game. He can sit down and enjoy it. 'What the hell are you doing up here?' I say when he appears for a third at bat. 'I don't like to play parts of games.' That's what he says. Who knows who was pitching by that time? Some shitfaced kid from Double A, I think. He's reading headlines—'SHIT-FACED KID KEEPS CAINE FROM .400.' Reality sets in quick. Chance muscles up and takes the kid over the wall. What else happened? Not much. Two walks and then the top of the ninth. I say, 'You know you only need a triple to go for the cycle?' He says, 'You're right, Bill.' Then the shit triples to center. Okay, tell me, who's ever been a better ballplayer? No damn body. That's who."

There were 50,000 people in the stands that day, and today, all these years later, there are one million liars who swear that they were among the crowd. Most of the liars were, in fact, listening to the soothing softly smooth voice of Beece Brewkley, longtime Lion radio broadcaster. Cloud floating in a half conscious state, relaxed and serene, summer hammock resting, mint julep vision in air, placed there by that voice talking, he was telling me Chance Caine stuff. Beece Brewkley was saying:

"I joined the Lion organization at the start of Chance Caine's fourth season, and I've been witness to Caine's magic for nineteen years. I broke in doing two innings and the post-game show. Then, after three years, I moved up to the top spot when Kenyon Young went to New York and the network. I've been so very fortunate to have been associated with high quality and highly interesting, sometimes peculiar, but never boring, people. There have been phenomenal teams here and yet, never during my tenure have the Lions seen a World Champions banner flying over Mander Stadium. Funny game, this. You've got to love it. I've been witness to so many great moments and met so many wonderful characters. Why, how can I forget Caine hitting for the cycle on the last day of the season to do the undoable, to hit .400 in the modern era. I recall Caine banging a triple in the ninth and Bill Able, who was the plate umpire that day, stopped the game, walked down to third base and shook Caine's hand. Then he gestured to the Lion dugout, indicating that Stony ought to send in a pinch runner for Caine. First and last time I ever saw an umpire make a substitution. Stony went along with it, too. The fans cheered for a long time. They knew they had seen something extremely special, and they tried to hold on to that moment. Caine had to come out of the Lion dugout a half dozen times to receive the plaudits of the fans. And remember Caine was the visitor, the enemy, in the Braves' house.

"With highs like that and many others, there have been lows, too. That Red Pugh home run. I had to call that one, and my heart was breaking. Boy! That was something! I have memories of Stony chewing umpires, Caine turning rockets into outs before you could blink, the most thrilling double plays performed, yes, performed by Sister Sepp and Caine, the Hal Bennett September, two perfect games by the brilliant Rainbow Clouds. Plays made by Fritz Fenneman, Sepp and Caine in Rainbow's second perfect game were heart-stoppers and came one each in the seventh, eighth and ninth innings. Fenneman's backhand spear of a slasher down the line was the twenty-seventh and final out. The Lions almost didn't have a third baseman the next day. His teammates had practically killed him jumping on top of him. Then Rainbow picked him up in his arms and carried him off the field. Yes, sir.

"When I sat in a little tin booth and announced all of my high school's football games, my dream was to be exactly where I am right now. The dream doesn't change. What great fortune for me that I still love what I am doing after all these years."

The first things needed to build a legend on the order of Chance Caine are a sperm and an egg. These items were supplied by Joseph Caine and Nancy Owens, respectively. Now we're digging back to see if there was a large orange baseball moon hanging in the western night sky when Nancy Owens Caine brought forth her son Chance. Did a parade of grizzled infielders arrive on the maternity ward to worship? Did the ghost of Honus Wagner slowly, ritually pass a bat back and forth over the sleeping babe? The mother doesn't recall any of that, but she does remember her husband, Joe, and how she met him. She is straight, tall, trim, whitehaired; has sunbronzed skin, a face with a lot of smile wrinkles, sparkle eyes that crinkle when she laughs. She said to me:

"My boy Chance is what my dad wanted me to be. It's sad that he died when Chance was three years old and never got to see him play ball. He was proud of me, though. He taught me to play ball when I could barely walk. I played baseball with the boys and was the only girl on the team. I played shortstop and batted leadoff. I was a runner. I could move. When I switched over to playing girl's fast-pitch softball when I was thirteen, it was basically because godawful puberty had set in, and the boys and girls were lining up on opposite sides of the field to plan battle strategies.

"Oh, I was a worldly high school senior. Ever so intelligent, cool, sophisticated, stupid. I was star shortstop on

the Sungold Orange, the best women's fast-pitch team in
California. It was a Fourth of July weekend tournament
in San Jose where I met Joseph Caine. There was a
green grass hill behind the fence in back of first base, and
on it sat scattered groups of people, fans, families, babies.
And all by himself at the top of the hill was this guy, with
long brown legs crossed and black curly hair, face buried
in a book. I remember he had on white shorts and looked
good. No fat on that boy. Looked like a runner. I spent
more time looking at him and trying to figure out why he
was there, since he never took his nose out of his book to
look down at us, I mean me, playing this oh so exciting
game. I ripped one between the outfielders to drive in the
winning run in the bottom of the tenth. Then I looked
over to the hill to see if he had noticed, but he was gone.
We had an hour break before we had to play again
across the park at the main field for the championship. I
zonked out on my back resting in the shade under a tree.
'You played a very nice game' are the first words he said
to me. I opened my eyes. He was crouched there beside
me, smiling at me, book in hand. Well, I tell you. My
eighteen-year-old heart began to pound. I was sure he
could hear it. I certainly did. We talked for fifteen minutes. By that I mean I talked for fifteen minutes. Blah,
blah, blah. Tried to impress him with the 'going to study

English Lit at Stanford in the fall . . . lucky enough to win a scholarship . . . me . . . I . . . my . . . me . . .' When I finally wound down, he wrote his name and address on the back of his book, then ripped the back cover off and handed it to me. He tore the cover off! I stood there. 'Look me up,' he said. 'I'll be glad to help you settle in. I teach Sociology at Stanford.' A tremendous gulp. My face went red. And so on. When it came time to play the game, I played it on wings high above cloud number nine. This time he watched. The damaged book was on the ground beside him. His arms were folded around shins. His chin was resting on his knees. I can see him there forever. I went to Palo Alto in September. I looked him up. We went jogging together, at least. We were married at Lake Tahoe on Christmas day that year, much to the agony of my parents. Chance was born the following September, much to the ecstacy of my parents. I lost my dad when Chance was three and my mom when Chance was five. My Joe fell down and died when he was only 47 years old. But I'm still here, pushing on."

In Chance's green diary, the one he kept during his final season, there's a remembering Mom passage. Let's do the obvious. Put it here. The hero wrote:

My mother was the ballplayer in my family. My first memories are of me hanging on chain link fences and people telling me to get my fingers out of the fence or they might be smashed. My mother, the shortstop (what else?), smiling at me from the field in her powder blue uniform. My dad always sitting in the stands with his legs crossed and his head craned down into a book. I remember brightly colored uniforms all around from games completed, games in progress, games yet to be played. My mother in the on-deck circle blows me a kiss. Her teammates shout, 'Come on, Nance, start us off!' She's the leadoff hitter. She can really run."

Why does Chance Caine love baseball? Simple. He was breastfed in a dugout. Why was he so physically gifted? Ma's genes? But what if I told you a story? Let's say one day, sitting on a hill in the park next to the ball field, legs crossed, head bent in deep concentration on his book, Joseph Caine heard from the field, where a line drive foul ball had been hit and was speeding directly at his head, the cry, 'Watch out!' He looked up at the last instant. His hand moved and the ball was caught and sent rolling back down the hill. He shook his red palm. Someone yelled, 'Sign him up!' The quickness of hand, Chance Caine's trademark, was a gift from Daddy. I could tell you that. It could be true.

Chance's green diary. The last year. One part says,

> My dad was only 47 when he died. That left my mom. Got no brother, sister, uncle, aunt, cousin. In-laws are out-laws now. But I'm here. I am the best ever to play my position. But the skills erode. I read Blessee's obituaries every day. For once he's right. Need somebody. Ever hopeful is this boy.

Chance, your old teammate, Lou Copter, might have told you to be careful of the smoke. But hey, let's not dwell yet on the depressed forty-year-old playing down his final season's days. There's more hero's youth, when the legend was formed. There's even basketball.

6

The Jekyll-Hyde Thing

Do you remember when piano man Van Cliburn and his hair took Russia by storm? When diva divine Maria Callas took down Scarpia? When Spencer threw the grapes in Ingrid's face? When Hepburn and Grant, disguised as Susan and David, were roaming the night hunting a pet leopard? Been in the California lettuce-growing country where the hunchback's son was looked after by the penguin, full moon or not? Been on the castle grounds where Orson's model ruled? It's the show biz twisting and intertwining into something like reality. Edith Piaf Marcel Cerdan Jake LaMotta Raging Robert DeNiro not to mention his father which brings us into the Rothko Rauschenberg and so forth and so on thing.

As I wandered in the local mall playing the above offshoot of the linklink game, something intruded into my consciousness just as I was drifting off to a side contemplation of Fatty Arbuckle and Virginia Rappe, the 'starlet' whose life ended as a result of Fatty's appetite. I was taking a break from Chance Caine, his life and times. The ageing poet that is I became aware that my body was swaying and my head was nodding to the 60's mega big Beatles singing 'Hey, Jude.' The 'dadadadas' were coming from the Muzak speakers. I made a note to add a new thing to the good side in my getting old ledger. Right under 14) The perfect harmony of comfy chair and satellite dish, I'll put 15) The Muzak starts playing your music.

Cool, efficient, serene. Chance Caine on a baseball field. When I had the big umpire, Bill Able, on the phone, he filled my ear with an unending cascade of Chance Caine stories. The one that goes here says:

"Chance Caine? Businessman. Perfect gentleman. Never gave us men in blue any trouble at all. I'll tell you about Chance. I got my break to get into the big leagues by replacing a dead man. That's right. Danny Hafford called a guy out in Pittsburgh, then fell on his face dead. Shit. Uneasy time for me? 27-year old ass-faced kid in the majors scared shitless and happy excited and scared to show it 'cause I'm traveling around with Hafford's crew, and they ain't in the most joyous of moods, having just buried Danny.

"Oh, they test you. They test new meat. We umpires are very special people. Don't let nobody kid you. We have to take a lot of shit. They test you until they know your shit limit. Holy Christ, lemme tell you, they tested my ass. In triplicate! And I was fogging guys out of games day after day. Pretty soon a guy'd just naturally scratch his ass or something and I'd wind up and fog him out of there because I interpreted it as a death threat on my infant son or some damn thing like that. Brogie from the league office talked to me, and my partners talked to me, but I was still a tightass.

"One day in August the Giants are playing the Lions. I'm out at second base, close to nervous breakdown and ready to crawl back to Albuquerque. But shit, I tell you something happened. Chance Caine played that game like a goddam Horowitz. He owned the goddam game. And it rubbed off on me, for Christ's sake! I grew calm and settled comfortably into the flow of the game, riding Caine's coattails. The game slowed down.

"I saw everything. I moved perfectly to my spots, had perfect position, saw every play, made all the calls. The

Lions lost on a bottom of the ninth homer, but god damn shit, as Chance jogged by me toward the clubhouse, he said, 'Nice game, kid.' Hey, the guy had noticed that I was along for the ride as he worked at playing his game perfectly. From that game on I was a damn good umpire. Still am. He called me 'kid' that day. He was right. But shit, you know, he was only twenty-three years old then. I was twenty-seven."

Chance Caine on a baseball field. Cool, efficient, serene. But in an earlier time, maybe the stiff staring great big dog with the yellow eyes stood in the road to the top of the hill. Perhaps Chance held his bat out pointed at the bristling neck hairs, the rumbling growl, the lowered head. He might have been calm and moved slowly, keeping the bat between his eight-year-old body and the dog. Could he have eased over the hill and as he went down, the horizon rose up and blocked out the yellow eyes? Let's say that the boy Chance knew the tree-lined streets, the alleys, curbs, lots, fields, holes in the ground, rotting old houses, rotted board fences, the weedy creek winding behind back yards and under streets to the bay. Let's say he knew the hills where the houses got fewer and trees and brown dust greenery made a wilderness to crawl through.

The green diary does some memory wallowing:

> I hate artificial turf. When we play on it, I feel like a miniature mechanical wind-up toy. Artificial, fake, unreal. Baseball is a green grass game. When I was a kid, I used to roll madly down the hills at the community park. The green, well-clipped grass of that place is one of the most vivid memories I have. There's a smell to it, too. The Little League field where I played was in that park, and I was there easily six or seven hours a day every summer when school was out. We'd play for hours, Bobby Ullett and Chance Caine, then just sit on the grass, sweating in comfortable exhaustion. Walk over to Sim's Market. Drink root beer.

Well, what does all this have to do with Jekyll and Hyde? I'm getting to it. Don't worry. I do have a plan—a kind of blueprint in my brain. We've got a blissful Norman Rockwell childhood for this guy. And he goes on to super efficient under control focused excellence on the ball field. The brilliant Dr. Henry Jekyll. So where's Eddie Hyde? Bobby Ullett can take a turn talking. The lifelong pal. The best friend. He can say:

"Did you know Chance had academic and athletic scholarship offers from all over the country? The athletic ones weren't for baseball, either. What do you think of that? They were for basketball. What a player he was! What a shooter! What a defender he was with his quickness. We had all our success in high school with basketball. We were tough in hoops. We could play. At 6'3" I was the tallest guy on the team. We won with full court man to man face to face all the time all out pressure defense. Chance must have averaged something like 10 steals a game. Coach Vade ran us, ran us, and ran us. Nobody liked to play us. Weren't no fun for them."

And now, maintaining the flow, the coach talks. Vince Vade says:

"Chance Caine could have played pro basketball. There is no doubt in my mind. Around here they still talk about the teams he was on. The kids now won't run like they would then. Shoot, they wouldn't have run then either if they hadn't seen Chance wind sprinting, wind sprinting, wind sprinting, again, again, again. They got right in line and followed along. He had the work ethic. He was a leader. They followed. The result? Toughest damn little team this area has ever seen. They could run backwards faster and longer than other guys could run forward. Everybody hated to play us. The good teams could hold together for a half, but the pace and pressure inevitably wore them out to the panic of exhaustion. The cheap shots of frustration my boys learned how to take. It broke my heart that Chance turned down UCLA and North Carolina to play baseball. His father wasn't too thrilled, either. Chance followed his own heart and his mother's, if you ask me. Who can argue with the results?"

Not me, for one. But it might be amusing to ponder some what ifs. What if the major sports hadn't bloated out and overflowed into each other's seasons? What if Chance had played basketball and baseball? A point guard-shortstop combo double Hall of Famer? Chance doesn't think so. His Hyde approach to basketball wouldn't let it happen. That's what he says. Like this:

> The difference to me between basketball and baseball? In basketball I needed the frenzied crowd in a packed gym to get me excited. I could play baseball anytime, anywhere, in front of anybody or nobody. It didn't matter. I used basketball back then to express adolescent anger at the lack of total universal perfection. I played it to beat and humiliate, not to display my superiority, but to display the other

man's weakness. Loved to steal the ball, drive down, fake through your face and score. People don't like to be humiliated, particularly when they are 16-year old males in the United States of America, or any other place, for that matter. . . . So I had my share of late night post-game parking lot fist fights. I'd be dead today. We only used fists then. Okay. I chose the right sport, the one where I played against the ball and not against my fellow man. What a bunch of crap! Nevertheless, I think it's true. Sad to me, too, that my friendship with Bobby Ullett is undeniably deeper because he was always there by my side in those post-game fights. We were US. They were THEM. And Alice was uncontrolled passion after I fought. I guess she was a fight fan. But I wasn't. Am not. I chose the right sport.

Sure you did, Chance. But the bench clearing brawl is not exactly a rare phenomenon on the major league ball field. What did you, Chance Caine, do when the bodies surged to meet at the mound in a melee of flying fists and tackles? Once, I have heard, a bat fired at the base of the mound jumped up and tapped Rainbow on the shins. Players, coaches, managers erupted onto the field swinging, kicking, wrestling, biting, gouging, building an animated angry pile of humanity. Chance, you walked into the dugout, sat down and watched. There you are. If it's a basketball brawl, you're at the bottom of that pile, kneeing and gouging for all you're worth. A baseball bench clearer? You're above it, outside of it. You step aside, wait for it to end. Wait for the interruption of your game to be over. Wait to get back to your position with one out and a runner on first. Chance could shrug and say, "That's the way it's always been."

The polite good sport is pretty much a yawn. So I probably should be picking at the broken marriage and at the basketball teenage anger stuff. I can't talk about the gun or the pretty lady yet. So let's try the basketball first. Listen to Vince Vade, high school coach, reliving the best memory he's got. He says:

"You coach a lot of years. You coach good teams and bad teams and in-between teams. You see everything happen from miracles to pathetic displays of weakness. You always look to somehow build a team unity, so you can come up with a whole that is more than the sum of its parts. When you get a team with that kind of unity plus the talent, watch out, you will be dangerous and difficult to defeat. But always remember one thing. Most of the fine teams, the great ones, the ones that click, end their seasons with a loss. That happens to be the nature of the animal. You have to be able to deal with defeat. Because at the end, there is only one winner in that final game. I have had my share of fine teams, but only once did I get to that final game and win it.

"Chance Caine, Bobby Ullett, Clifford Jones, Carl Emrich and Pete Sandpiper. José Leon and Steve Kinder off the bench. The Magnificent Seven. That's what they were known as in this town. They won it all. Undefeated state champions. They were the best I ever had. They worked hard, drove themselves. And they fit together beautifully. And the talent was there. Chance had the most. That has to be obvious, since he's the reason you're sitting there listening to me drone on about a high school basketball team that played decades ago. But you can't go 33-0 with one man. I don't care how good he is. We had seven players who contributed strongly in different roles. Bob Ullett was our 'big' man at 6'3". But he was a full physical man, 215 pounds of muscle and leap. Cliff Jones—speed, jump and shoot at 6'2". Carl Emrich— long arms, dogged defender, at 6' the key to our press along with Chance. Little Pete the playmaker. 5'6" maybe on a tall day. Great ballhandler. He and Chance could get through any press, and did. José came in to spell Pete or Chance and was a deadly long range shooter, like Chance and Cliff. Three great shooters. And then there was Kinder to come in for up-front strength. A football lineman with some quick.

"I don't care who we played against. What I remember is the team functioning so smoothly and in control always, whether the shots were falling or not, whether they were calling garbage fouls on us or not. The poise, the total confidence and cool of the group during time-outs with the bands blasting and the fans roaring. Only the last four games were close. I had the heart attacks. The kids yawned. We're trailing by eight to start the fourth quarter of the big one. Pete Sandpiper says, 'No sweat, coach. We've got 'em.' Their emotions were under wraps. Well, excepting Chance. Those other six boys, who were really men, played basketball like Chance played baseball. All business. No great displays of emotions. But Chance was a whirlwind, attacking, attacking all the time on offense and on defense. He could embarrass his man. Steal a ball, score, shake a fist in a face. Oh, sure, a contrast. He carried himself so completely differently on the basketball court than he ever did on the baseball field."

Okay, that's enough basketball coach talk. My job, as I

see it, is to stagger around in Chance's youth trying to do some damn thing or the other. People are saying "Talk to this guy, talk to that guy" and I talk to this guy and to that guy and get some stuff which might be something or might be nothing. What do I know? So in the course of events somehow I find myself sitting in a real estate office and two guys are talking at me. One is the Pete Sandpiper guy from Chance's high school undefeated hoop group. The other guy is Mel Finch, who had played against that team. Both these guys are white shirt, tie and ample waistline people. Mel Finch says:

"Chance Caine and basketball, huh? The way I thought about him? He was a human buzzsaw who needed his face caved in. You could have got a lot of volunteers to do the face cave back then. First time I played against him, I started up the court one time with the ball and he stripped me clean, scored, turned to me and snarled, 'That's one, pal.' I couldn't wait for baseball to smash him. They had a shitty team except for Caine and their lefthander Bobby Ullett. I was a pretty damn fair pitcher myself and I wanted to see Caine in that batter's box. I sat him on his pants first. Then I struck him out with my change. I yelled, 'That's one, pal.' He laughed, said 'Nice pitch' and jogged back to the dugout. We played them twice and creamed them twice my junior year in baseball. Both times Caine was a smiling gentleman. End of the season rolls around and I like the guy. Next winter we come to play them in basketball and my pal Caine is again asking for his face to be caved in. Following spring, he's Joe Nice again. I'm glad he made it in baseball. He wouldn't have lived long if he'd stuck with hoops. Somewhere along the line his face would have been caved for good."

Let's leave it to the shrinks to babble about why Chance Caine played basketball one way and baseball another. Do I personally care? Not really. But I am an admitted liar. In any case, moving along, it's Pete Sandpiper's turn to talk. Are you ready to hear him relive his winning shot in that last game of that perfect season? Too bad if your answer is no. Sandpiper closes his eyes, leans back in his chair, hands clasped behind his head, and says:

"The play was designed to get the ball to Chance, but when he moved behind the pick, he hit a wet spot and went right down. I was stuck with the ball and the clock was going. I had to shoot it. A kind of over the head set shot throw. It released perfect, and I knew it was in. I have never ever forgotten what a wonderful feeling that was. It was the best moment of my life, riding on that surge of screaming joy. The Shot, I call it. The Shot has helped me over some rough spots in my life. When I'm down, when something goes wrong, I close my eyes and I can see it happen again, the ball hanging at the top of the perfect arc, then falling with its rolling backspin through the hole. The net barely quivers. The goosebumps rise again."

Thanks, Pete. Get a life. Now it must be noted that there has been much moaning and groaning about how Chance Caine and his Lion teams never won a World Championship. They are generally acknowledged to be the best team that never won the final prize. Not the feather in your cap you want. Chance mused on the subject in his green diary. After some blather, the part I want to put here went:

> Come to think of it, I do have one championship. A high school state basketball championship. Not a World Championship, but I think for the 12 of us, for Coach Vade and for every student in our school, the success was as sweet-tasting as anybody's victory anywhere in sport. Red Pugh, running out his homer, couldn't have felt any more joyous than Pete Sandpiper felt after canning his game-winning 20-footer at the buzzer. The peak is the peak. Can't get higher.

There's that name Red Pugh again. We'll get there eventually, if you don't know already. It's no great crime not to know. It just means you aren't a big sports fan. Then why are you reading this? That's another question. You deal with it. I've got enough troubles of my own. My first slim volume of poetry, *Patchquilts*, sold enough so that my second slim volume of poetry, *Patchquilts II*, appeared shyly on the scene. You see. There you are. I explain myself in my titles. If you are confused about what is going on, try thinking of the word 'patchquilt.' See if that does anything for you.

Now about Chance Caine, I am going to say that he has known the thrill of ultimate victory once on the basketball court and thousands of times on the baseball field. Get it? Having said that, this chapter is declared officially over. Except for what Roland Pfennigmensch, Chance's Little League coach, had to say:

"Chance Caine and Bobby Ullett. I picked 'em both as 9-year olds for my Little League team. Bobby Ullett was going to be the major leaguer. That's what everybody thought. Turns out he was one of those kids that mature early physically. When those two boys were nine, they looked like David and Goliath standing next to each other.

"Chance was a little squirt, but he was totally in control, completely unafraid. Couldn't hit the ball much further than the edge of the outfield grass, but oh, could he pick up those ground balls. His mother knew a lot more about baseball than I did, and she drilled her son so he knew what he was doing out there. If we coaches would have opened our eyes, it would have been clear to us what boy was the major leaguer. He had perfect hard working attitude, brains, and was always a glove magician. What he didn't have was size and strength, and that was all he didn't have. Well, those two items eventually arrive through time and work. For Chance, they came in a sudden burst in his junior year in high school. By the time he was a senior, you were watching a major league infielder. It was the most natural thing in the world. Chance Caine was an under-sized shortstop at a school with a terrible baseball program. Three years later, he was National League Rookie of the Year. Boy, did that put a stop to the second guessing around here about what a mistake he had made not to go to UCLA or wherever on a basketball scholarship. Yes, he was awfully good in basketball, too. Coach Vade was the best, and what a gift it was for him when Chance came back to school as a junior four inches taller and a lot stronger."

⑦
Sidebar

A Baseball Nickname That Doesn't Work:
Edwin 'Running Bag of Offal' Tenutti

This little chapter is in here for flavor. It's a bay leaf or some oregano kind of deal. It's not going anywhere, but it's here. The Alice stuff is a downer, but hey, that's life in the poetic composition game. I didn't promise you an A-Z narrative. I've got to throw in some 3s and a few #@s along the way. Such as perhaps maybe Brillo Pete Jacoby, popsicle-cleaning man, wanted to start a rose garden. Became an aphid farmer instead. Sold crushed and blanched aphids to health food stores as an aphrodisiac.

Sorry. That bent way too far into nonsense.

So Flappy Byness has been called a racist. He denies the thing. Says to him it's neither fish nor herring. Says any young man who plays baseball for him is judged on how he plays baseball for him. The only exception to that is drugs. The young man with the habit of drugs he does not want around.

He considers the young man with the habit of drugs to be a weak failure who will do nothing but rot away the quality team. In the Lion organization, if a young man is found to be using drugs, he is through for good. There is no second chance. Flappy states that he is not a racist, but he supposes it is true that he is a druggist.

Chance modeled his public speaking style à la Flappy Byness. Chance never knew what to say on the banquet circuit, not that he really traveled the banquet circuit. But when he was in his home territory in front of a bunch of kids and dads, he had no planned presentation. Then he hit upon the idea of pretending to be Flappy. All he had to do was collect the clichés and unscramble them. He could then easily get through a ten-minute talk and a question-answer session. He compiled a good batch of Flappy stuff and sat down in the hotel one day to sort it all out. Flappy's pronouncements were always obvious and a shade strange. They were also right! Laugh at what he says, but he's flat out right! So Chance copied Flappy whenever he had to make a little speech. Honesty, hard work, and not screwing around. That's their motto—

Flappy's and Chance's.

To the double space above I add, as added emphasis, an announcement that by veering sharply to the left, I tell you that Chance Caine did write in a letter to his wife when the marriage lay in ruins, "Every time you break my heart, pieces of it are lost and it grows back smaller." That's the best line he ever wrote. I know it is because I've read all his scribbles while in the process of trying to build whatever this is. It's his only scribble I wish I'd written myself. I don't know why Alice, the ex-wife, let me read that, and I don't know why Alice, the ex-wife, said to my face:

"I don't know why you think this is your business or anybody else's business, but all right, for once and the last time, this is it. According to my mother, I could never do anything right. My father died when I was five. When I was fifteen, I found another father, Chance Caine. I wrapped myself into him. He was quiet, serious, above it all. You know . . . Chance Caine. Except when he played basketball. Then he was on fire, angry, like me. I loved that.

"He loves baseball. So he played that. Is this some

great revelation? No? We got married and had lots of money and a beautiful custom built home and we lived happily ever after. Only we didn't. I never had the slightest desire to be a mother. Except maybe to my hydrangea or my hyacinths. Freak woman? I am a not unsuccessful landscape designer. My partner Roger and I have all the work we want. The only clause in my divorce that was important to me was the one which gives me the right to go out to Chance's house and oversee the care and feeding of the grounds and gardens. Nothing wrong with Chance. Nothing wrong with me either. Now. Things are different. Things didn't work. Okay. Move on. Let's leave it at that. Do you have enough now?"

At that point, her partner, who had been standing next to her during her whole speech, flared into life. He sputtered at me, "Alice married a man who plays a game, and he wasn't what she needed. God. Why can't you leave the lady alone? She needs not to be bothered by you. Kindly leave us in peace."

So I left them kindly and in peace. When I got home and to my material, I dug around and found a Nella Vade reminiscence tape. Nella Vade. You know, the high school classmate of Alice and Chance. The basketball coach's daughter. I played the tape of her showing me through a yearbook:

"This is me in my senior year. That's me, the P. I was a very important letter. If I was sick and didn't show, we spelled out IRATES instead of PIRATES. Not really. We had understudies to go on in our place. Imagine, being an understudy letter P. Now here's Alice Rowe, all serious in the Poetry Club. The flash picture of her that you would get from anybody in our class is her leaning against Chance in the hall and looking into his face with moon eyes. You're talking to one retired letter P who dreamed from afar to be in Alice's shoes."

Maybe not such a great dream. Hold on! Wait a minute! Let's crash out and journey to Clichéland, where following a winning Lion effort, announcer Beece Brewkley interviewed Chance Caine. This is really boring, so I'll try to keep you awake.

ON THE RADIO

BEECE BREWKLEY   Welcome to the Lions' Wrap-up Report. I'm Beece Brewkley, and my
(yawn)   guest today is Chance Caine, who delivered today's game-winning hit. Congratulations, Chance.

CHANCE CAINE   Thank you, Beece.

WHAT CHANCE SHOULD HAVE SAID   Your fly is
open, Beece.

BEECE BREWKLEY   Well, that was one big win for the
(time to   Lions. It puts a little breathing room
count clichés)   between you and those pesky Giants.

CHANCE CAINE   Every win helps. We saw in the
(woo,   seventh that the Giants had lost and knew
insightful)   we had a good opportunity to pick up a
                 game on them.

WHAT CHANCE SHOULD HAVE SAID   Pesky? Didn't
he play for the Red Sox?

BEECE BREWKLEY   Now tell us about that hit in the
                  ninth. The bases were loaded and they
(blah, blah,   brought in this new boy Horton who had a
blah, blah,   great Triple A campaign. Did you know
blah, blah)   anything about him or had you ever faced
                  him before, perhaps in spring training?
                  What were your thoughts in that situation?

CHANCE CAINE   I did face him a couple of times in
(this defines   spring training. He's got a lot of talent.
boring)   Throws very hard and finds his zones. He
                  had nowhere to put me today and so he
                  had to throw strikes. I was looking for a

hard one anywhere I could hit it.

WHAT CHANCE SHOULD HAVE SAID   The kid was nothing. I knew the game was over.

BEECE BREWKLEY   He got you 0-2 before you
(wow)   connected.

CHANCE CAINE   Right. He dropped a curve on the corner that I wasn't expecting. Then he
(whew, don't   came in with a fast ball and I pulled it too
overdo the   much. The next pitch was a good one, a
humble bit)   hard slider down and in. I had to golf and was lucky enough to dump it into right. The kid is good though. He showed me a lot.

WHAT CHANCE SHOULD HAVE SAID   I let it go to 0-2 to get the crowd excited. I could have gotten a hit with the handle end of the bat.

BEECE BREWKLEY   He is big and can throw it through a brick wall. Chance, when we come back, I
(goll!)   want to ask you about that collision you had with Fritz Fenneman.

CHANCE CAINE   Okay.

WHAT CHANCE SHOULD HAVE SAID   No.

commercial

★ ★ ★

another commercial

★ ★ ★

one more

BEECE BREWKLEY   We're back talking with Chance
Caine, the Lions' All-Star shortstop, and I
(see the   want to ask you, Chance, about the
concern   collision you had with Fritz Fenneman
dripping off   going after that popup down the left field
that voice)   line. You both are okay, I hope.

CHANCE CAINE   Oh, yeah. We're both fine. It wasn't
that bad a collision.

WHAT CHANCE SHOULD HAVE SAID   Fritz got
kneed in the nuts, but he's fine now.

BEECE BREWKLEY   How did it happen? Normally the
(impeccable?)   communication is impeccable out there.

CHANCE CAINE   Well, to tell you the truth, we were
both going hard after the ball, and we
(ha, ha)   weren't worried about crashing together.
What we were concerned with was the

whereabouts of Cliff Pinney. Fritz was racing out from third, I was coming from short, and we knew Pinney was on the move from left. A collision with Cliff Pinney is something you just don't walk away from. So we both were tracking the ball and looking for Pinney, and we forgot about each other.

WHAT CHANCE SHOULD HAVE SAID   You play the game. Shit happens.

BEECE BREWKLEY   I don't think Flappy felt too well when he saw you two sprawled out there in left.

CHANCE CAINE   That's probably right. But we're okay
(truth, justice   and Fritz caught the thing. That's what's
American way)   important.

WHAT CHANCE SHOULD HAVE SAID   Who cares what Flappy felt? How do you think we felt?

BEECE BREWKLEY   Thank you, Chance. Congratul-
(wrap it up,   ations on today's win, and let's keep the
babe)   momentum going through September.

CHANCE CAINE   Thank you, Beece. We're going to try.
(aw, shucks)

WHAT CHANCE SHOULD HAVE SAID   Thanks, old
man. What do I get for being on the show?
Not another shoe certificate, I hope.

⑧
Verna

What do you start with when you sit down to write? That is the question? Not to be or not to be, but what do you start with? A what if? A factual incident? An idea? A concept? Or is there suddenly a string of words that rub nicely together? An opening sentence in the "It was the best of times" or the "Call me Ishmael" vein'? A beauty of a "yes I said yes I will yes" final sentence? You start any way you can. I, in fact, have a story title sitting in my head right now that must be dealt with eventually. It is

Green Moon's Run

It swept into the brain and perched. From where it came is one of those fun little mysteries that I can't solve. There was no "Xanadu Kubla Khan" opium dream involved. I stumble around this world in a sober stupor.

And the day after the title came to me, a first sentence walked in and sat down next to it. It read:

If you can reach the highest place, you can look down and see where the story ended.

Here is the assignment. Finish the story. I've got more Chance Caine to deal with.

Following a close loss during the pressure-packed final days of a pennant chase, Flappy Byness closed the door to the clubhouse. He himself came out and made a short statement to the gathered media. "Gentlemen," he said (though there were three women in the room), "when the cows come home to roost, we'll be there waiting." He then turned, went back through the clubhouse door, and locked it behind him.

Chance's diary, the important one, the one he kept during his last season, falls open to the following entry when tossed lightly onto a couch. It also doesn't open at all or opens to boring passages when tossed lightly onto a couch. But finally, perseverance being rewarded, it does open to the desired place, and the old weird poet that I am is made to be calm. And here is what Chance wrote:

My body was temple of my spirit. Spirit's gone. Ball I used to stand in front of skidded by the old glove. Could not get there. Could not reach it. The one I used to stand in front of. It went by me. Another thing. I should have screamed that pitch on a hop to the wall in right center. My pitch. The guy made a mistake. Right down the fat it came. I put the bat out there. But late. End up on second base okay, but the hit, it was a flare, a corkscrew dubbed out to kiss chalk on the left field line. Tied up the game, though. Kept it going. Drove in the run. But the question is what's going on? I say yes to a young girl in the hotel lobby. For more than two decades I've been visiting museums, going to movies, reading books when on the road. I never cared or noticed about the eyes going if you read too much. I read too much and look at the lifetime batting average. .335 is not sneezing fodder. It's Hall of Fame fodder. That's what it is. That's what she said. The girl. I want you because you're going to be in the Hall of Fame. She said that. I didn't say much. But I didn't walk off like I usually do. I talked to her. Why? I tell her to come back to the hotel after the game. Dinner, etc., I tell her. Good, she says. I will hit one into the ivy for you then. This I say. I am crazed. Something is wrong. New things to try. Never told Alice I'd try to get a hit for her. Sentimental crock.

If I give it all up, maybe I'll be a hermit poet. This is the last season. The ball went by me today. The one I should have been standing in front of. And my double to left should have been off the wall in right.

The green diary speaks, and having spoken, now rests on top of my desk clutter. So, Chance, you devil, an out-of-wedlock liaison with a luscious young thing. Shocking. The first time in twenty years? The first time ever? You did focus pretty much on the old ball game, didn't you?

I'm a liar. I've said that, haven't I? Good. Well, the girl in the lobby had a name. And the name that she had was hers, and it was Verna Peckham. She was born the year Chance came up to the Lions. He was her daddy's favorite ballplayer. She was eight years old when Chance chased and caught a .400 batting average. She sat on her daddy's lap when he was listening for reports on the radio to tell about each time Chance came up to bat and what he did. Chance went four for four. After he was two for two his average reached .400, but he refused to come out of the game because he said Ted Williams didn't sit it out when he hit .400. Verna said her dad thought Chance was the greatest player of all time. He used to say to her, "They don't make them like that anymore." He told her that Chance gives the game his entire self, mind and body, from the time he puts on the uniform until the last out is made. Not like the rest of the candyasses out there for money and showbiz. Verna and her dad came to town every time the Lions played the Cubs. They sat behind first base so that they could watch Chance play shortstop. When Chance jogged to the position, her dad didn't look anywhere else. He saw what Chance did on every pitch and explained it to Verna. When an Academy Award was given to the documentary film of Chance Caine fielding, play after play, slow motion, freeze frame, with Beethoven's "Moonlight Sonata" caressing the eardrums, Verna and her dad saw the little clip that was shown during the Oscar broadcast. Verna's dad went nuts. He jumped out of his chair. "We gotta see that, Verna!" he yelled. The next day he was calling the movie theaters and saying he had to see *The Fielder*. He got steered to a film society screening in Chicago, and he brought Verna up and they saw the whole thing. Verna's daddy said it was the greatest thing he'd ever seen. Verna was only ten, but she thought it was great, too. That's when she really fell in love with Chance Caine. In that little dark theater on that slow motion movie screen with the Beethoven music playing in the background. She followed Chance's eyes following the ball he had sent toward first base. A quick nod of his head when the ball beat the man. The camera stayed zeroed right in there on his pretty eyes.

That's Verna. Chance's green diary continues:

> The girl was there where we'd agreed to meet. While we ate dinner, she told me her whole life story. Her name was Verna. She told me where she was when I hit the four triples in one game and what she was doing during the World Series we lost to the Tigers and old Stony Babcock. How she cried. How soft she was in my arms. She got dressed, kissed me once, and whispered "I hope I get pregnant" in my ear. She turned to the door, paused, came back. "Don't worry. You won't see me again. I won't bother you for one dime. I swear." She

looked me in the face. "This is all I wanted."
She walked out the door.

That's it? Chance, Chance, Chance. How are you going to appeal to prurient interests with a paragraph like that? Where's the stallion rampant? Where's the sword of love? Not to mention the quivering gasps of ecstacy that I'm just now mentioning? Well, it was bleak, wasn't it? Forty years old, wifeless, childless, career draining away, the last season.

> know me by number
> number's six six
> know me by name
> always it's chance
> know me by number
> number's six six
> know me by name
> chance you are through

ONE NEED NOT WORRY IF CONFRONTED IN THE LION CLUBHOUSE BY MEN IN UNDER-WEAR WITH NYLON STOCKINGS PULLED OVER THEIR HEADS AND BASEBALL HATS

WORN INSIDE OUT AND BACKWARDS. THE
PENNANT RACE IS ON. SHOES ARE NAILED TO
THE CEILING. JOCK STRAPS ARE GOING UP IN
SMOKE. AND THE HERO OF EACH VICTORY
GETS TO SMASH A PIE INTO THE FACE OF
BULLPEN COACH NED CRANLEY. THIS IDEA A
BLOSSOM FROM THE MIND OF CARL "FATHER"
FRISCH.

> know me by number
> number's six six
> know me by name
> always it's chance

awww, you know the rest   finish it yourself.

⑨

The Infielders

In my head I start with the silent movie *Greed* which takes me to Erich Von Stroheim who whisks me to *Sunset Boulevard* then not to Gloria Swanson Joe Kennedy again, but to William Holden. From this point there are many paths to follow. one goes from Stephanie Powers to *The Girl From U.N.C.L.E.* to Noel Harrison to Rex to *My Fair Lady* to Julie Andrews to *The Sound of Music* to Oscar Hammerstein to O What a Beautiful Morning. Another goes from *Stalag 17* to Otto Preminger to Gypsy Rose Lee to Ethel Merman to Ernest Borgnine to *Marty* to So Whadda You Want To Do Today? I Don't Know. Whadda You Want To Do? The link link game strikes again. I play this game a lot when I'm stuck. It takes me on peculiar journeys. Here, I'll tell you what. Let me place down at this time in this place a small segment of link which connects in a relevant manner to the subject of this growing stack of words. What a concept! Relevance! Here goes. *The 400 Blows* to Francois Truffaut to Jacques Michelle to *The Fielder* to Chance Caine. From here we can actually step into this chapter, which is supposed to be about the infielders who played alongside Chance as he built his legend.

I'm taking out the sketchbook for some quick draw impression factoid human being summaries of those infielders. You'll have to dig your own details later in order to judge how well I can draw. Some of these guys have better, juicier stories than Chance. Well . . . maybe not.

Get ready.

Get set.

Sister Sepp, ten years Chance's second base partner, said, "Chance Caine was not a humper. He steered clear of the honey doves. Talk about me I've sampled every rhea from dia to gonno and back again. But when the blueboy said play this game I used what I had to subdue the ball and do the win things. I was a flash. I gave off sparks. And in the night I belonged to the honey doves, and they took care of me. Oh, yes, they did do that."

The green diary of Chance says:

Time to get out the slippers and start spinning yarns. Mainly I had two second basemen to work with in my career. For my first eight years, Hen Philpott was the guy. He was a little stump, hairy, hard working, not afraid to make his living in the dirt. Master of being hit by pitches. We turned neat textbook double plays—field, feed and fire. Then they traded him away to make room for Sepp, your basic definition of a hot dog. And a great player. My partner for ten seasons. Then he went to the Yankees as a free agent. We turned the double plays. We turned them fast and beautiful and more than any other combination ever. A shortstop's greatest thrill? Turn two. The greatest play I ever saw? Sepp did it on the front end of a double play. Playing the Pirates, men on first and third, one out. Runner on first goes. I've got the bag. Batter, it was Dave Lake, rips a low line shot obvious base hit to the Sister's right. But Sister dives out full stretch. Bats the ball on the short hop WITH HIS BARE RIGHT HAND directly to me standing on second. I jump to avoid the runner sliding in and whip the ball to first. Inning over. Double play. Lake has not yet dropped his bat or moved two steps down the line. The Pittsburgh crowd was stunned, quiet. Then they started roaring. Sepp had to come out of the dugout, tip his hat, take a bow. Yeah.

Watching poetry. If it is possible to watch poetry, base-ball fans did it when they took in the Caine-Sepp show. The Caine-Philpott show wasn't shabby, either. Henry Philpott, Caine's earlier partner, said, "I enjoy the Old-Timer Games and go to a lot of them. I get a boot out of stepping onto that big league ballfield again. The way I look now gives the crowd a tickle, too. I don't mind. I earned my belly fair and square. Got a base hit this last year in Houston, too, and made a play at second. I sat around the clubhouse all day trading memories. Amazing how good we all were. How did we ever lose a game?"

When you need an analysis of the great Lion infields, you are required to turn to the highest authority. Stony Babcock said, "I take my Chance at short and my young lady at second. The Sleeper stands out there, and the other guy with the glasses is the third baseman. Earlier or later, it doesn't matter which to me, you or me or the rest of the guys over anywhere haven't seen more twinnies turned than by my group of gentlemen. That one is writ-ten down even typed in the book."

Fritz Fenneman, the third baseman with the glasses, contributing succinctly, said, "We had a good infield. Cable, Sepp, Caine, and myself. I doubt if there's been a better one."

At first base stood John "The Sleeper" Cable. I swear

I am not lying when I tell you that he said. "And should my brethren of the infield choose to gather in one place and bring forth all of their golden gloves, the very ground would yield to the weight. Fenneman, Caine, Sepp, Cable, for nine years we staunchly stood, an unbroken unit. Ah, baseball, my life's second choice. I would rather have pursued with diligence and perspicacity a career in the Kingdom of Nod."

After that statement fell out of the telephone into my ear, I needed help. I knew where to turn. I had to talk to Carl "Father" Frisch, relief pitcher and lay analyst. He said, "You walk up to John Cable and say 'Hello.' Then watch him search for about a minute for the perfect comeback. You know, this guy is one of the complete loon phonies of the world. He won't come out and play with us. He's hiding in there behind the gobbledygook and phony naps. In the batting cage you could watch him be mad. Mister Above-It-All bashed at the ball in slit-eyed rage. A member in good standing of the human race. You know. Stone cold bonkers.

"The other two guys on that Billion Dollar Infield with Caine and Cable were Sister Sepp and Fritz Fenneman. Now, Sister Sepp could play the game. He had the good brains, too, you know. But for him, everything, brains, talent, you name it, disappeared in a flash whenever he sensed female molecular combines in the area, be they plant, animal or any combination of the two. You got it. Another loon. The puzzle is Fenneman. Friendly, good guy. You can't come up with more niceness than he's got. So what's his problem? The loon factor has to be in there somewhere. You know, let's just call him a lunatic freak of normalcy. Right?"

So they called them The Billion Dollar Infield and these are their stories in a nutshell, collected and presented by me, your lying but amiable guide.

3B
THE ALMOST EXCITING STORY OF FRITZ FENNEMAN, BOY MAN

Fritz Fenneman was never a little sapling. He began oak-hard and remained so forever. He mushed through rain, snow, sleet, and the rest of the stuff to make his paper deliveries in a green green Seattle suburb. When he grew up to teenagehood, his football crash line backing and baseball ripshots made him citywide type of famous. University of Washington welcomed him to their football fold and there he battered West Coast ballcarriers. In the spring, he line-drived at the plate and dove at third to make the play. Oddly enough, his dog died on the day he signed the contract with the Lions. When he made the big club a year later, he had a new dog. He married beautiful Lee Ann. He watched his twins born. He remembered as the best life moments treks through the pines with his dog and sledding down icy steep Seattle street in the dead of winter with his sister Terri clinging to his back. Those were some good times.

SS
Guess who.

1B
A FEW WORDS ABOUT JOHN CABLE

Won a baseball scholarship to the University of Southern California. Likes to sleep.

2B
CHARLES SEPP BECOMES A SISTER

Easy. Raised by his sister. Called to her when small, "Sister! Sister! Wait for me! So the neighborhood called him 'sister.' A lot of fighting and hating and even a cut or two, but when the skills became apparent, the name became the style. Sister loves his sister. She's the only one he loves.

THREE TIMES HENRY PHILPOTT LET THE TEARS COME FLOWING DOWN HIS FACE

1. At the birth of his boy, who arrived with a wounded, malformed little head.

2. When his wife ran away from home forever soon thereafter.

3. When his fourteen-year-old boy, Tim, was rolled out of the operating room at the end of his eighth and final long surgery, the surgery that completed the restructuring of his face and delivered to him a normal appearance.

I'm not a liar sometimes. It's a fact. There are mountains of facts. You could get lost in the mountains. Or at least confused. There's THE World Series with Pugh and Babcock and Tigers. I'm not ready to tell that story yet. There's BIG DOINGS at the end of Chance's final season. I can't go there yet. There's mystery. There's romance. Dare I say love? Dare I say soul mate? I dare. But not yet. Let's examine more foothills first. There are trees to climb and creeks to cross. There are landscape metaphors to be escaped.

10

Good, Bad, Ugly, Normal, Crazy, Stupid, Loud

Rainbow Clouds, Kenyon Young, Tim Connell, Bobby Ullett, Lou Copter, Bull Ketra, Bill Able. Good, bad, ugly, normal, crazy, stupid, loud.

Two bunts, one slash, five swings and out of the cage. A batting practice sequence. What the heck, a life sequence. Two bunts, one slash, five swings and off the world. Geez, baseball metaphor! Met as in New York, a as in what you say when you don't know the answer, phor as in four or 4, being the numerical designation of the second base position. I'm hanging around this story and starting to sink into a kind of midnight metaphorical tar pit. Help me out, Rainbow.

Five years into his retirement, Rainbow Clouds appeared at Cooperstown to be inducted into the Hall of Fame. Both of his little daughters were wide-eyed and solemn sitting there feeling special in new dresses. Their mother sat next to them, and her eyes shone with pride. The Rainbow, introduced by former manager Flappy Byness, made his speech. It went:

"My name is Jesse Cornell. I have been given gifts by the Lord which have enabled me to lead a perfectly happy life. And I am not talking solely about my physical abilities. No, I am talking about the woman who married me and the two sweet children we have made together. I am talking about my mother. I am talking about my father. I have had opportunities given only to a few, and I hope I have taken advantage of them in the right way.

"I loved playing the game of baseball almost as much as my shortstop over there, Mr. Caine. Let me be Rainbow Clouds for a minute and say, I AM THE ONE AND ONLY PITCHER OF ALL TIME AND AVERAGED 25 WINS PER YEAR. ADD THOSE VICTORIES UP AND DIVIDE BY TEN, PEOPLE. Now let me be Jesse Cornell again, Josh and Emily's boy. If I had not had that man playing shortstop behind me for those ten years, I probably would have only averaged a measly 20 wins a year. I have a hunch that would have been good enough to get me here some day, but without Chance Caine at short, it might not have been today, and it surely wouldn't have been a unanimous selection, which I am very pleased that it was. I thank all my old teammates. I see Tim Connell out there. Thanks, Battery.

"But the greatest honor is this. To go into this place and to be put up there to stand with Jackie Robinson, to stand with Roberto Clemente, Willie Mays, Leroy Paige, and all the others and all the rest. I am very proud. Thank you."

Tim Connell gave me the short version of Rainbow's induction. He said, "It was a real moving ceremony. Rainbow gave a real good speech. As for me, I won't get near the Hall of Fame except as a visitor. But I can say I played for a lot of years on a team with two of the guys who did make it and are, in my opinion, among the top dozen players of all time. Hell, make it top five! Wait a minute! Ask yourself who's done it better, and you just might have to make 'em 1-2."

And Chance, too, had something to say in the green diary, the last season log, the final fling's musings, the chronicle of the end of a career. The passage dealing with Rainbow into the Hall of Fame speaks in Chance's pleasantly readable non-scrawl:

When Rainbow went into the Hall of Fame, I was there at the ceremony. He went out of his way to compliment me in his little speech. That was nice. Won't be long before I'm there giving my speech, will it? I've got five years plus a little to get to as nice a place in life as Rainbow has. The odds might be long, but I battle.

Okay. Fine. Now I'm going to introduce you to a new person. You might think you know him just because he's famous, but you don't. If Will Rogers had known him, he'd have met the guy he said he'd never met. I'm talking about Kenyon Young. I don't have to tell you about him. He'll be glad to do that himself. The stuff I have here all poured out of him as I sat in his glass cube of an office with a wall of television monitors shadow dancing behind me. My chair was hard, angular, uncomfortable. He was sunk back into the supportive cushioning of his recliner, eyes closed and babbling. He said:

"Don't accuse me of not knowing the American Dream. I married five of the most gorgeous female bodies you'll ever see, and I have three kids scattered across the country sucking money off me. I'm softhearted or softheaded when it comes to the other sex, whatever it is. Odds are good that I will give another one a shot at marrying me and my money yet again. Maybe this time I'll get one of them that knows how to do it. Enough of that. A Chance Caine book, eh? Well, I'll tell ya.

"My role in the world is King of Hype. The Lions' radio ratings shot up there when I okayed a deal to do their play-by-play. I got too good for them, so I left it to the cornball Brewkley and went to New York to run the whole sports arm of the network. I let New York beg a bit before I went. Had to have the proper coinage waiting for me. I'd just booted bitch number two and needed some cash to throw at her. I am worth every penny they pay me, and they pay me plenty. I deal only in fact. Saves time. Sitting around being humble is nothing but a massive waste of time. I rocketed the ratings through the roof, and that's where I kept them. I ran the Olympics good enough to get covers on *Time* and *Newsweek*. Got the praise. And rightly so.

"You've got to hype and showbiz it up because pro sports in America have been diluted to mediocrity. In baseball you've got guys who would never have made it past Double A sitting on major league benches. Maybe they don't start, but they sit there. And collect big bucks. In football, same thing. Guys who would have been breaking each other's teeth out in sandlot semi-pro are racing up and down on punt coverage before 60,000 sadistic fans.

"I stir it up to keep the unwashed masses tuned in to some of the boring trash I must sit through. Here's a thought for you. Earth abides, and mediocrity abounds. It's true. It's hard to be good, but I'm the only one around. I've got to do it."

I thanked Kenyon for the insight on Chance Caine's career and left the place. Kenyon Young. What the hell is it with Kenyon Young? Why did I bring him in here to clutter up my nice clean story line? I know the answer to that question. Your job is to remember his name. It's Kenyon Young. He has an important function at a key moment in Chance's last season. He's going to introduce Chance to someone. That's all I'm going to say.

Those little star symbols are there to indicate that though we remain somewhere in the middle of Chapter 10, we will now slant off in a different direction. The part before the stars was the Hall of Fame and Kenyon Young bit. The part that's coming up directly is pretty much entirely focused on Chance and Bobby Ullett, Chance's best friend since always. I'll start the part about Bobby Ullett after I trowel in this pertinent quote from the big umpire, Bill Able. He has stated, "Dumb shits, smart shits, stupid shits, total shits . . . baseball's got 'em all just like any other life. But down under, I'd say the majority of the men in this game are okay shits." That said, we move smoothly on.

Bobby Ullett played semi-pro baseball when he was nineteen, twenty years old. The manager of the team was a serious-as-hell red side of beef named Bull Ketra. Not only did he think he knew it all, he thought he'd invented it in the first place. "Turned purple four times a game at least screaming at the umpires, even if we were ahead 14-zip," says Ullett. Once threw a kid named Don Brook, a little second baseman, against the fence for missing a suicide squeeze sign. This Ketra's a jolly chap. One day somewhere along life's highway, schedules happened to hit right for Chance to get down to see Bobby pitch in a tournament. The Lions had played the Giants in the afternoon. Bobby Ullett was pitching for Blue Tree in the evening. It was a Saturday. Most of the players taking part in the evening matchup had played with or against Chance at some previous time. But Bull Ketra had never met him to talk to. According to Bobby, "Bull invited Chance into the dugout, glued himself to his side and spouted non-stop into Chance's ear. When we were up, he peeled himself away to take his place coaching third, but kept darting his eyes back to the spot where Chance and I were sitting. I poked Chance to demonstrate to Bull that he wasn't a mirage. Chance asked me if Ketra was as gross an abomination as he seemed. I said he was grosser. But what the hell. Big Bull's only another dreamer. And on that night he was as close to his dream as he'd ever be, sitting next to it in a dugout on a choppy field where he's managing a bunch of half-good, half-ass players playing baseball, hardball, for the love of it. The fat jerk." All right, right then and there, I get the picture of why Ullett and Caine are pals. One little interview. Kee-ripes, close your eyes and you can't tell which one's talking.

I bet Bull Ketra would say, "Pus arms. All my players got pus arms. The fields stink. There's no maintenance. Try to get the city to do something. Fat chance. It's a joke. I could have a good ball club if it weren't for the pus arms. Where am I supposed to practice? Goddam soccer teams running all over everywhere kicking balls up and down every field every day all year in their underwear and stupid hair. How can you run a program? How can I have a good ball club with a bunch of ignorant pus arms? Who wants to work anymore? Nobody. Pus arm bastards." That's what Bull would say. Maybe he said it.

Bobby Ullett knows Chance Caine better than anybody else. They've been close like brothers since they were nine years old. They were thrown together at nine

118

when they were chosen to play on the same Little League baseball team. They were the only two nines on a club with mostly big strong scary elevens and twelves. Bobby says, "I'm a lefty with a strong arm. That's reason enough to draft a nine-year-old. I say that since I've been managing Little League myself for years now, and I know what I'm looking for in a nine. Chance and I, thrown together by our mutual nineness, warmed up together, sat together, played together and stayed together as buddies. Chance's mom, she was something! A hell of a ballplayer. She took us out, pitched batting practice to us, hit us flies, grounders. She was tough. She made us work. In our Little League games that first year, I played minimally and served my time in right field. Chance played every game the whole game at second base. At ten, he moved to shortstop and stayed there forever. At ten, I moved to pitcher-first baseman and stayed there through high school. After high school, I've managed to squeeze in semi-pro ball, marriage, mailmanship and fatherhood to fit along side the slow-pitch softball where I still dig the dirt balls at first and send long, high drives to challenge the cyclone fence in right. Yeah, slow-pitch. Good legs and belly-over-the-belt time."

People talk to me. I don't know why. Do I look like an ear, a kindly giant receptive encouraging ear? Bull Ketra said, "Pus arm bastards are all a bunch of hot dogs who couldn't cut the mustard." Chance talked to me, gave me his most private thoughts in his green diary. The diary rambles and muses over times spent outside the lines, the lines that tell you if you're standing in territory that is fair or foul. Says the diary:

> My pool is three meters wide and twenty-five meters long. Five meters of it are under my roof, and I walk up out of my pool into my living room. The one thing Alice and I did together nice was to design and build this house. December is my swimming month. I submerge inside my house, then swim outside into storms. Crawl laps for an hour out into the storm and back and into the lightning and back. Then in to shower, dry off, sit by the fire and stare into the storm. That's about as dangerous and thrilling as the old life gets.

Green diary doesn't know what's in store for Chance down at the end of that last season. But most of you probably do know. You think this whole book is aiming at that extra surprise Chance received on Chance Caine Appreciation Day. You might be right. But sometimes famous events aren't the most important events. In

Chance's story, there is another thing that happens. This other thing that happens is the real reason I agreed to write this book. Stay tuned.

Chance and Bobby Ullett went backpacking in the Sierras back of Yosemite every year the day after the Lions' season ended. That meant late September to mid-October, and a few times they caught some early winter, but more often enjoyed perfect, peaceful, quiet, mellow times. They walked along the granite, up and down the meadows, across streams, sometimes going three or four hours without a word. Chance carried his glove in his pack, Ullett his big floppy first base scooper. They stopped out there on the back of the mountain and played catch. That's when they talked. Chance rehashed the season, and Ullett gave him the word on the hometown happenings. It was a ritual. Bobby Ullett told me, "We had one fine time. It was slightly different later because my kids came with us. I jerked 'em out of school for a few days. Joyce—that's my wife—she liked being rid of the whole bunch of us for a little peace and quiet. She hated camping, and that's a fact. My kids adored Chance. Mister Uncle Magic Famous. He played catch with Molly across a stream. Fell in once to get a laugh out of her. We had some hellacious ball games with pine cone and walking stick."

In the green diary, Chance is blue. The last season is crawling to a close. Then what? The diary says:

> My high school team was never too successful. Bobby Ullett and I were the only two on the team with more than adequate talent. Bobby was a lefthander, threw hard, had brains. He is still my closest friend, and I envy him his good marriage, his kids, his pot belly, his comfortable fit into life. Wow. And me? I've got my glove. Stubby fingered. I know I feel the ball in my hand the way the old ones did. The gloves now, the ball in there is just a rumor until you dig it out. I have framed and on the wall in my house an old faded newsprint photo of Honus Wagner, waiting in the on deck circle, leaning on his bat. A tough, thick, powerful man squatting there with big strong hands and wrists. He knew the bite of the ball in the cup of his hand when he picked off a hissing line drive. My hand is calloused in my black oiled glove. I wonder if it is like his. I think so. I am of his time. I am a horse and buggy man in a rocket to the stars world.

Pay attention, Chance, and listen, people. Having done some research, I have found out that America, when it greeted the new century, dressed up in red, white, and blue. The Pittsburghs of the National League had a second-place team with Honus Wagner playing right field and winning the batting crown at .381. Three years later, Wagner was at shortstop, and Pittsburgh won a pennant.

Now quickly to the green diary:

> Transport me back to the times when the stands were filled with guys in straw hats. Give me a little scrap of glove, and stand me at shortstop. Bat me twenty years next to Ty Cobb in the order. Almost 8500 hits between us. Imagine riding the trains. Playing the game.

When I gave Lou for Lunatic Copter his SuzyQs under the bridge, he thanked me by saying, "It's hard to breathe. Too much smoke. It's not the games that are of any importance whatsoever in any way. It's other aspects. They are of minimal importance to you. They don't matter. I know the important things, and they don't matter either. No one knows the right things. I know some of them. The world is through. I can't be touched. But you don't care. It doesn't matter to you. THEN GET THE HELL OUT!!!"

chance
you want to go back
play
in the dusty heat
of the century
new

But wait. What about the horseshit in the streets? The lack of air conditioning? Wouldn't you miss your satellite dish? Your jacuzzi? Well now, Chance, I've got to admit that I don't think any of that stuff would bother you.

⑪
Tips from the Pros

You find some freaky things when you rummage through the baseball dross looking for amusing items. There was a catcher named Foote and pitchers named Face, Hands, and Fingers. Look it up. The one called Fingers had a tie-her-to-the-tracks-I've-got-the-mortgage mustache and was a ninth-inning-get-the-last-outs pitcher like Carl "Father" Frisch. Try to make a body-part team. Too many pitchers. Not enough infielders and outfielders. For instance, Head was a pitcher, too. It's a lot easier to make a team of colors with all the Grays, Greens and Blacks. You can even have a Blue-Green battery. Something to do while you're waiting for life to happen to you.

Fingers was a mustache man. I'm a mustache man, too. I once sported one of those Norwegian face framer beards and endured a naked upper lip. I stayed with it for a few months, but decided eventually that it wasn't the look I wanted for the me that is I. The bald dome, modified walrus mustache image I now project makes me look less like a member of Lincoln's Cabinet and more like a turn-of-the-century barkeep. I can live with that. Do live with it. Like living with it. Are you waiting for Tips from the Pros? Relax and wait no longer.

In the hot drive to the pennant one year Lion pitcher Randy Kepp threw an important two-hit shutout, snapping a personal four-game losing streak. After the game, discussing his effort with the scribes, he said, "Tonight I just went out and threw hard. That's the difference. The past few weeks I've been aiming the ball. Tonight I said the hell with it, I'm going to reach back and fire. I only threw five breaking balls all night. The rest was heat and a few straight changes. I didn't get cute out there. That's been my big problem. Too much thinking."

Two years later, in another drive pennantward, Randy Kepp tossed a four-hitter to keep Lion hopes alive and notch his 18th victory after having been stuck at 17 for three weeks. After the game, discussing his effort with the scribes, he said, "Tonight I finally started to think out there. I went for the spots and hit them. Lately I've been trying to blow the ball by them. I haven't been thinking. Tonight I concentrated on putting my pitches in good locations. I had them off stride, and I didn't overthrow. You don't have to throw it through a brick wall to get outs. You've got to think out there."

If you really want to hear about it, they'll talk. The pros, I mean. About the game. About how they play it. What they do. Analyze, dissect the situation, the elevation of the arm, the angle, spin, compactness, bat speed, the hand position, posture, extension. They'll talk about the fine tuning of details that smooth the flow of the game. Nelson Pick, the old Lion pitching coach, started with the basics. He told his pitchers, "I'm going to tell all you guys the same thing. So remember it. Your arm is not attached to me. I cannot feel it. I do not know when it is hurting. Don't hide nothing from me. Your arm is your paycheck. Don't abuse it. Treat it very affectionately. Be its friend. Your arm is in your hands. So pay attention to it." Sound advice from a sound mind.

Carl "Father" Frisch, pitcherslashphilosopher, had the right mental approach for a closer, the guy who has to get that last out in a nasty situation. He said, "You know, I got a philosophy to live by. It goes, 'Expect to be screwed.' If you aren't, you'll be pleasantly surprised. And if you are, you'll have been expecting it, and it won't bother you all that much. Right? Let me admit to you right here that I've been more pleasantly surprised than screwed on this go-around on the planet. I'm just a pleasant young chap serving my time in this galaxy. So I know that giving up a game-losing hit is not that big a deal, universewise. After all, you know, we're just playing glorified wiffle ball on this speck of dust whirling in the void. Right?" Possibly.

I'm not sick of being a liar, but it's time for some real truth, some history book verifiable info bites. Now listen to this. In 1876, George Armstrong Custer and his monumental ego set out to subdue the troublesome Sioux Indians and their pals in southern Montana. He and his men died at the Battle of Little Big Horn, where the warrior Crazy Horse and the medicine man chief Sitting Bull outthought and outfought the doomed yellowhair Custer and his bluecoats. Chicago second baseman Ross Barnes hit .429 to take the National League batting title and, along with the tireless battery of 46-game-winner Al

Spalding and catcher Deacon White, led the Chicagos to the pennant by six full games over the St. Louis team and its one-man pitching staff, George Bradley. Look it up. A little perspective for you on the antiquity of the game. For a long time they've been figuring out how to do it—what you have to do. Techniques, basics.

Jared Hudson was the batting coach when Chance Caine materialized as the Lion shortstop. He said, "You spot flaws in a youngster's swing. You try to correct them. You try to develop the good habits, mechanical and in the head. You say the same things to hundreds of young men. You live for the few who soak up your ideas in a flash and have the skills to execute. That first spring training, when Chance Caine came up, he lost his front shoulder all the time. I spent two twenty-minute sessions with him, and he's got that shoulder compact and huggin' in. Instant perfection from both sides of the plate! Damn guy should have hit .400 for his career instead of just the one year. But he didn't love it. Didn't put in the time. Rather be out there pickin' grounders."

If there is any significance to the fact that a few pages in Chance's green diary have entries written in green ink, I haven't any idea what it might be. One of the green ink entries is this one:

As far as hitting goes, that's been the work part of this game for me. I could always hit anybody's fastball anytime. My quickness and strength down through my arms saw to that. But until Jared Hudson got me to keep my front shoulder in there until the last possible instant in fact to turn it in even more as I strode to the ball I was a feeble waver at off speed stuff. Okay. Here's the formula to hit .400: front shoulder in, weight back, God-given eyes, God-given quick in the hands, and tremendous focused concentration. I had that last item only one year. The year I hit .400. Hitting is not my passion. Has not been. But I was swept into it with all the hoopla, and I saw a solid goal sitting out there. To hit .400. So I focused in and made my assault. That was the time this game became work. The spotlight on me big. I maintained the Chance facade of cool pretty well, and I hit .403.

I bet you knew that the stock market crashed in 1929 and the Depression was on. I bet you didn't know that Lew Fonseca nudged Al Simmons .369 to .365 to nab the American League batting title. The National League champ was Lefty O'Doul, who missed .400 by a hair, finishing at .398. President Herbert Hoover would stagger through a few more years. FDR was warming up in the bullpen. You see, this stuff has been going on for some time.

More green ink in Chance's diary:

> Every 500 games I take a rest. Who needs to worry about a playing-in-so-many-consecutive-games streak? The only time I ever missed more than two games in a row was when my hamstring got torn. Lost two weeks there, and the whole team went to pot. Fistfights. Stony fired. Flappy hired. So I thought I'd better stay in the lineup to keep the turmoil at a minimum. I guess I've missed about forty games in 22 years.

There's a space of about two inches, then this, still in green ink:

> They ask me how I make so many great plays. I'll tell how to make great plays. I've been thinking about it since they asked me. To make a great play, you must go all out on a ball you know you can't possibly get. Sometimes you get it.

I have reached a conclusion of the green ink portion of

Chance's diary. I'm going to say he found the pen in a hotel room on some road trip as he rummaged around looking for something to write with. The pen that went with the diary had turned up missing, as is sometimes said. So he dug through drawers and came up with Mr. Green Pen. Who cares? Get on with it. This chapter does have a formal ending.

You can read it after you finish reading this sentence.

the game
is old
and new
the same
and not
it is
a messenger
from
then

⑫

The Green Diary Talks

But first, I've got in front of me a Chance Caine rookie trading card. There's a roaring Lion logo interrupting a cloudless sky in the upper right corner. Across the bottom, below a blue, batting-gloved hand holding a two-toned brown ash bat which is resting on the right shoulder of a creamy white home jersey, there is printed in gold letters outlined in black CHANCE CAINE SS. The face under the hat staring at me from the card is youthful, pudgy and serious. You can't see the number on the jersey. It isn't 66.

Now the green diary talks, and says things like:

You get used to the number that you wear on your back for a lot of years. I wore number 17 during my rookie year. Not many people can tell you that. Good trivia item. I liked that number. It was the dream to play in the major leagues realized, made solid to hold in my hands. And every time I put on that shirt with the big script LIONS across the front and the big 17 on the back, I moved in my mind to a place of comfort and well-being.

Somebody had the bright idea after I was such a hotshot rookie to give me number 66. So I've worn that number for 21 years. I've gotten used to it, and I like it now. I like the nickname "Boxcars." I like to hear it.

But my real number deep inside is 17. It's been worn by five or six others since I had it. Somebody else may wear it, but it's my number.

There is no mystery whatsoever as to who had the great idea to make Chance Caine's number 66. It was Everett Mander, owner of the Lions and famous short jugeared billionaire with high pitched droning monotone voice. He pours the story himself at every opportunity into fresh ears. His long suffering secretary Madge pivots and retreats if she enters his office and hears, "I believe I made Chance Caine the youngest multi-millionaire there ever was." At least that's what she did when Mander started telling me the tale. He did say, "I believe I made Chance Caine the youngest multi-millionaire there ever was. I exclude of course people who inherited wealth, such as myself. That contract was a big story back then, and I made it bigger when I changed Chance's number. I thought 66 was a perfect fit for him. Had my reasons. Made it happen. I handed the new jersey to Chance at the press conference I'd called to announce the new contract. Nice shot for the photographers. Writers wrote a lot about the new number and the new contract, which had of course been my target all along. They speculated that 66 stood for 66 million.

"I let them. They knew only that Caine had signed a lifetime contract. I told them that 66 was selected to be worn by Caine in honor of the fact that he was better than any two other shortstops put together. I let them take it from there." The little chromedome then leaned back in smug contentment reflecting on his puppetmaster brilliance. I needed to talk more with him, but I really wanted to be out in the adjoining room with Madge discussing secretary stuff.

The green diary on Chance's number. You've had that. It's a story. The green diary on Chance himself. Self analysis of the guy. It's there, too. It starts with a Ben

Blessee reference. Remember Ben Blessee? No? He's the sportswriter who wears loud coats, writes bad columns. In the diary:

Ben Blessee is always giving me knowing winks. Knows nothing about me, but gives me knowing winks. He thinks he's my mentor or some damn thing. He embarrasses me the way he's always writing columns about what a great player and man I am. He's right about me as a player, but he doesn't know the first thing about me as a man. As a man, I don't rate myself particularly high. What I do is play a little kid's game. I was no good at my marriage. On the other hand, Alice was rotten at it, too. I possess great rage. Not many have witnessed the cool facade of Chance Caine boiled off. My rages do not happen on the baseball field. They're homework. Like the time I killed a dog when I was out jogging in the hills. I wrote a poem about it:

i killed a dog quickly quickly
while i jogged a path near home
he had leaped through air to get me
strike me, crash me down
quick quick quick i break the neck
the broken body falls

and now jog on along the way
with open mouth
suck air

Two hours later, sitting in my house, sitting in my empty house, I felt rotten. I still feel it. As a man, I'm not all that great.

Lighten up, Chance boy. The dog jumped you, didn't it? It was a fair fight. You won the hand-to-paw combat. Give yourself a break. As far as I know, and I know far, nobody has a bad word to say about you. Not even Alice. Oh, yeah, except a few elderly former high school basketball players and Cliff Pinney. Your teammate Cliff Pinney. He gave you a black eye. You came out of your clubhouse once with a black eye courtesy of Cliff Pinney. What's that story? I know what the story is because Cliff Pinney gave it to me himself. He said, "Chance Caine is a fucking robot. You know something? He never gives no shit if the team wins or not. Damn cool bastard. Hell, I ain't saying he didn't always put out his best. Course he did. He's a windup toy. A robot. Shit yes, I fought him in the clubhouse. We've just lost the seventh game of the playoffs, and we are gone. It's a morgue. Except for him. He's damn near showered and dressed. The rest of us are sitting around too used up to pull off our uniforms.

Our heads are down. And he's just going about his business like nothing. It just pissed me off. Just goddam flooded mad through me. So I yelled something at him. Then I shoved him. Then I punched his fucking face. The bastard did nothing. They pulled me off. I was going off, screaming, kicking. The son of a bitch said, 'Nice season, gentlemen' and walked out. Goddam robot shit. Don't get me wrong. He's a Hall of Famer. What happened is buried. That's a while back. He made plays I still don't believe."

What do I think Chance Caine would say about Cliff Pinney? There is nothing in the green diary to quote. I haven't done the research. I haven't asked. So I make it up. But it could be true. Educated guess and all. Chance, a half-hour after having been punched, would have said, "When somebody hurts me, they don't exist anymore. Why think about them? I can't talk about Cliff Pinney because as a human being he does not exist for me anymore. Wipe the slate clean. Delete him." That's what he would have said then.

This chapter is way too depressing. We need something brighter. An injection of humor. Since I am in charge, I will drop my Billy Little quote in here. Billy Little was the team trainer for the Lions during Chance's entire career. He talked Chance with me and said, "Chance

Caine was never hurt. He never had nothing. He had a hamstring once for a couple weeks and then one other time he had a ankle for a few days. Other than that, nothing. Because he stayed in shape. That's why. He took care of it. The body. Simple. You want to hear about a guy? I'll tell you about a guy. Harry Jones was the guy. Get him a hotplate and he'd never leave the training room. This guy had a ankle, a thigh, two shoulders, one of each, a foot, two toes, a hand, and four knees. He looked like the return of Dracula's mummified daughter after I got him wrapped up to go out and play." Thank you, Billy Little, a man with a body, two arms, two legs and a head.

Now back to the misery in the green diary of Chance's final season. The diary speaks:

> One day I look up and I'm old enough not to be drafted to fight in wars. You know, what gets to me is when I'm just trying to live and go forward and I've got all these threads attached to me and a lot of people out there I don't even know are grabbing and pulling and tangling themselves up, rolling around and dragging in different directions, tugging at me, the annoying jerks, and if I try to throw them off, the threads wind tighter, thicken into ropes and

more unknowns stick a hand in and grab on for the ride. The weight of the people hanging is dragging me to my knees. If someone throws me a rope, I don't know if it's got another hook to dig into my flesh or if it's really a safety line. Can't tell the difference. Couldn't. Alice— I never did have an idea of what went on inside her well-guarded fortress of a mind. But, a ball rocketed to my backhand I can snare on the short hop and feel the comfortable tug in the web of my glove. Grab it, set and throw before any man can blink. Hear it pop the mitt over there. The man is out. Sit him down. I can play this game. I know what to do. And can do it. I own the game. I am the best ever to play my position.

Look who's miserable—the man with all the money you or I could ever want. Gee whillikers, money can't buy happiness? That's a new one. When I was sitting under a freeway overpass next to a stinking trickle of a stream talking to the former Lion center fielder Lou Copter, he gave me a swell present, a nugget of truth, an enlightenment. He said, "You're still here. You can't take a hint for an answer. That's all right. The energies of my thought processes can deal with you. Not that you are of any importance at all. Though you are one of them out there doing things in the smoke. How do you do it? I wonder why you don't stop spewing from that slit in the middle of your face about Chance Caine. I know enough about Chance Caine. I don't want to talk about Chance Caine. WHAT THE HELL DOES IT MATTER!? WHO THE HELL CARES ABOUT CHANCE CAINE!? YOU'RE DYING!! YOU'RE DYING!! YOU! . . . ARE! . . . GOING! . . . TO! . . . DIE!"

It's always refreshing to be reminded.

For Chance, his career flicked by clickety click: base hits, liners, long run foul flies hauled in down the line, quick turn and hold the runners, body set to throw, off-season coldness, the wife goes traveling, spring training fresh, popping the sweat, squinting in sunlight, stretching for two, eating the ground balls, eating some more, nice new clean uniform, shiny new shoes, down through September, a pennant there this time, champagne will flow, but in Detroit waiting, the blow by Red Pugh, and on to the mountain and home to the empty and on to spring training and on through the years and up to the days that grow fewer and fewer in the last year you played.

But hope springs you know what (eternal, right?) and here is hope:

on the late summer road
the last summer road
in new york city
caine on the bed
eyes closed
asleep
the tv
is on
perfume commercial
world famous model
classic tall beauty
her name is
o'shea

Red Pugh Swings His Bat

Lions	AB	R	H	BI	Tigers	AB	R	H	BI
Sepp 2b	4	1	2	0	Quilp cf	4	1	1	0
Caine ss	3	0	1	2	Consigliari rf	3	0	1	1
Cable 1b	4	0	1	0	Todd 3b	4	1	1	0
Pinney rf	3	0	1	0	Pugh c	4	1	1	2
Fenneman 3b	4	0	0	0	Mahout lf	3	0	0	0
Harris lf	4	0	1	0	Escuela ss	3	0	1	0
Hermosa cf	4	0	1	0	Wapshot 1b	3	0	0	0
Connell c	4	1	0	0	Cheever 2b	3	0	0	0
Kepp p	2	0	0	0	Lyman p	2	0	0	0
	32	2	7	2	Stegner ph	1	0	0	0
					Ward p	0	0	0	0
						30	3	5	3

```
Lions     000  020 000 — 2
Tigers    100  000 002 — 3
```

Game-Winning RBI—Pugh. E—None. 2B—Cable, Caine, Escuela. 3B—Quilp. HR—Pugh. SB—Sepp, Todd. Sac—Kepp. SF—Consigliari.

	IP	H	R	ER	BB	SO
Lions						
Kepp (L, 2-1)	8 2/3	5	3	3	0	9
Tigers						
Lyman	8	7	2	2	2	4
Ward (W,1-1)	1	0	0	0	0	0

T—2:18   A—53,089

The time has come, I think right here, to speak of Red Pugh's blow. We'll turn and face that bygone day and leave Chance Caine to dream. While clearly on the TV screen, O'Shea, the smile, the hand, I'll tell you that it hurts them still, the Lion fans who wept. Can you read a box score? If you can, you know. You know the kind of story. Red Pugh's Blow. It is a myth legend bottom of the ninth, seventh game of the World Series story. It is Stony Babcock's revenge, Red Pugh's glory, Randy Kepp's defeat and a lot of other stuff.

It is Stony Babcock saying, "The Lions have a owner who as a cash register works good but comes out puny as a man. That's in reference to the previous times when we have been eating from the same side of the dish and he threw me overboard to where I landed in the tra la la land of Tigers and came back to get him in the Fall Classic. I take him in seven games in spite of the fact that the shortstop's not to blame and everywhere I look he's catching the ball or hitting it in the empty spaces and my pitchers are looking at me what am I supposed to say? When my catcher fat bats one to the depths and it looks like we might be incredible to win I'm taking one last look to make sure the shortstop can't get to it anyway even though it's over the wall and I am the one and only World Championship victor. I make a pretty curtsy to the cash register jockey, blow him a little kiss."

It is the ever present, ever annoying columnist Ben Blessee writing:

FLAPPY'S FAILURE
by Ben Blessee

Detroit—Merkle, Snodgrass, Owen, step aside and make some room. Flappy Byness has failed to issue an intentional pass to Red Pugh, and therefore they are dancing in the streets of Detroit town. Caine has been slain by his own manager.

The inning was the bottom of nine. The lead was one. The outs were two. Barney Todd, grim and determined, singled to right off of the tiring Lion hurler Randy Kepp. Red Pugh, Tiger backstop, walked to the plate, carried by the shrieking frenzied fans, clinging with mighty roars to the hope. Strike one. Kepp found the knees on the outside corner. Strike two. A mighty swing at the up and in. Todd races for second on the next pitch, which is low and away. Catcher Connell bats it down, makes no throw. Todd slides safe at second. Crescendo of frenzy in the stands, rising, maintaining, as Byness trudges to the mound to talk to his gallant pitcher. Oh, the fatal error. Byness returns to the dugout. Connell squats behind the plate. No! First base open! Walk baseball's home run king! But no. Flappy had told his pitcher to get him one more strike. It has yet to be recorded. The ball seemed to barely clear Chance Caine's leap, then rise, rise, rise to disappear into glorious Tiger history, and the world erupted.

Red Pugh, spinning airborne pirouettes, living

the greatest moment of his life, circled the bases through the mob. And as the whirlwind Pugh passed shortstop, Chance Caine, Series Most Valuable Player for the third time in three Series, amazingly all lost by the Lions, waved a salute to the victor and in his heart must have wondered when it would be his turn.

It is Lion broadcaster Beece Brewkley whose trademark home run call was "Good-bye, ball!" He used it on every homer he witnessed with one exception. When Red Pugh swung and connected in the bottom of the ninth of that big fat game, Brewkley announced, "Swings . . . It's a drive . . . Oh God . . . Detroit wins! . . ." Then he let the Detroit noise surge and said nothing, couldn't say anything. Felt like he'd swallowed his tongue and several lead ingots.

Okay. What about Chance? What did he feel? There is a green diary reference to the Red Pugh thing squeezed in amongst some of his negative self-analyses. In handwriting that goes from neat to scribble, he wrote:

Getting to the World Series three times was fun. There's a lot more hoopla and excitement, but they're still just ball games. Lions never won any of those Series. But the win-lose thing never gave me any great grief. You know, when Red Pugh pulled his childhood dream bottom-of-the-ninth-seventh-game-of-the-World Series-trailing-by-one-run-game-winning-homer, I didn't feel I was a loser. What I felt was that Red Pugh was a winner. Of course, Blessee went on for days moaning about what it must mean to me and my psyche to lose three Series. Don't mean a damn thing to me, Benny. But he doesn't ask. Just pontificates in print. Gives me knowing winks. Squeezes my neck. Poor guy doesn't understand the game. Has no clue. The thing I have for this game is the ability to play it close to perfectly, mentally and physically. I will step away clean. Now. Things I used to do I'm not doing any more. I won't be Flappy Byness or Stony Babcock, clowns, cartoon characters, threshing, digesting, being digested by baseball, baseball, baseball. I need a new direction.

Patience, Chance, we aren't to that chapter quite yet. What we need to do now is hear from the man who threw the pitch. Randy Kepp said it like this, "Instant numbing sorrow . . . a deepfelt sense of complete failure . . . a bulky clumsy body hard to control . . . somehow walking a narrow silent tunnel through color carnival joy . . . somehow moving to the clubhouse . . . sitting slumped at my locker . . . motionless stare at the details in the leather webbing of my redbrown glove . . . in my head again and again I throw the pitch and want it back . . . the crack of the bat . . . my disaster . . . pain . . . failure . . . beaten . . . hurt." Don't worry. Kepp didn't go the Copter route, didn't end up picking through garbage cans for nourishment and income. He dealt with it.

And Flappy Byness? He said, "What can I say without adding more? Mr. Kepp had the man. One ball and two strikes. Three strikes and you are out. He is a Harvard man. He said he could get the corner with his slider. I believed he could. Sometimes a slider don't slide. That's it."

The umpire Bill Able will talk loudly on any subject, and this one is no exception. He told me, "All right, what would they be saying if the 0-2 pitch was handleable and Connell had gunned it down to Sepp, and Sepp had put it on Todd's leg for the World Series ending out? Stony Babcock would be the senile fool. Sending a man on an 0-2 pitch with two outs trailing by one in the last inning of the World Series? Insane! But he did it, got away with it, so they chuckle at the crafty genius. And Flappy? I admire his ass. He weathered the shit well, almost like an umpire. Pugh's a basher, yes. But Kepp had handled him easily the whole Series, whiffed him four times. So when all the shit about percentages and strategies and charts and histories are chewed up and down all day long, it comes down to the simplest of statements. And Flappy Byness made that statement. He said, 'Sometimes a slider don't slide.' The other manager pulled the screwy play, but he won the damn game. There's your difference. Shit, Flappy's team stretched that Series out to seven games without their two-time 30-game winner, Rainbow Clouds. People keep forgetting that."

Yes, but maybe Stony was crafty. Maybe he knew what he was doing. Maybe he was a student of the game. After all, it was his life for hundreds of years, wasn't it? So, with that in mind, when Stony says something like "That Harvard man gets a guy 0 and 2 and you know something about him is that you could calculate he'll try to get you chasing dirt on the next pitch so you wonder why you won't send your runner down to steal second base?" maybe we should believe him.

The Lion players from that team spend their lives answering questions about that game. What did it feel like? Were you sad? Sister Sepp: "No problem. That's fates. Folks can't carry my glove got the big time ring. Means the ring ain't no big thing." Cliff Pinney: "We were one of the best teams in the history of the world that year. If Rainbow's there, we smash 'em in four. Shit. It don't matter anyhow. Except that we were the best and we lost." Fritz Fenneman: "I took my dog and drove off to the mountains and fished, listened to the river and walked around with Babe. That's my dog. More or less got back into touch with what the world really is where I like it. Felt a lot better, too, when I came home. Still hurts, though, in my gut, when in my mind I see that ball disappearing over the goddamn wall."

Carl Frisch, the relief pitcher, was a rookie on that team. He talks. He muses. He tells stories. He drew the picture like this, "Well, sir, you know, I was warming up, and I was ready. I couldn't stop throwing though, because I had to keep moving. Then Flappy went out to talk to Randy. I stopped throwing and began to do my mind focus. I wanted the ball. Then Flappy went back into the dugout, didn't call me. So I switched my mind focus, you know, and sent waves of positive vibes out to Randy. Suck it up, Kepp. One more wicked nasty. That's what we called his slider. No man in that bullpen was moving a muscle or even breathing. The people were standing and screaming as Randy went into his set position. Deafening. Then the noise tripled when Pugh swung. It was not to be believed, you know. My life sagged. My body was heavy unset glue. Movement to the clubhouse happened. I don't know how. I sat, like everyone else, drained, too beaten to move. We looked like propped up dead men. It was quiet for a long, long time. Well, you know, that was how my rookie year came to a close. I wasn't a rookie any more."

Bob Ullett was the one who talked to Chance about the game a few days after Red Pugh connected. He heard the story sitting on a granite slab near a river high up in the Sierras. Ullett told me, "Several years ago on one of our mountain trips, the one after that awful Series, I talked to Chance and asked him why Flappy Byness pitched to Red Pugh with first base open. We were fishing a quiet pool in the river. I want to say first that I have been a Little League manager for a long time, and if anybody knows the second guessing shoulda-oughta know-it-alls sitting in the stands, it is a Little League manager. That's the thing about baseball. Any ignorant slob can be an authority. It's an American right. Shoulda bunted. Shoulda been playing on the line. Shoulda been deeper. Shoulda taken him out. Shoulda left him in. Should never position your right fielder there with a 2-0 count on a lefthanded batter with only one out. That's the way it is. The shoulda that popped out at Flappy Byness in knee-jerk reaction across the nation was 'shoulda walked him.' After Red Pugh's miracle homer, the after-the-fact masterminds speak out loud and clear. While I'm thinking about it, let me tell you what a buddy of mine did a few years back. This was a guy who had played with Chance and me in high school. He wasn't much good, but he became a good manager and teacher in the Little League. The stands where the parents sit are right behind the team's bench at our park, and this one year the he-shouldas and why-doesn't-hes muttered and mumbled behind his back finally finished my buddy. About the fourth inning of a game halfway through the season, he turned around and stated in a conversational manner to the main mutterer, 'The team's all yours.' Then he walked away, got in his car and drove off. Never came back. To coach, I mean. Now he helps me with my team. But only at practice. He's not interested in going to the games. So here I am with all this background and what do I do up there in the mountains with Chance Caine? I ask the question. Why didn't they walk Pugh? Chance answers: 'Because we hadn't been informed that he was going to hit a homer.' "

⑭
O'Shea

Romeo. Juliet. Sandwiches. Ice cream. What's in a name? Billy S., who might have been a competent second baseman for Stratford-on-Avon had history taken a different turn, asked the question. What is in a name? Bags of stuff. I've been going through this baseball lore and names I never knew existed have jumped out at me in full bloom, with personality, standing in the community, be it high or be it low, wardrobe quirks, facial tics, peculiar ways of holding the hands above the waist just so. Like Hod Eller. Hod Eller! A name. A pitcher. A picture. Hod Eller should be my favorite baseball name. But it isn't. Nor is it Ned Garver. It's not Eddie Plank or Dave Concepcion. Or Stony Babcock, even. It is a cup of coffee relief pitcher name of Chuck Churn. I can't explain it.

It shouldn't be. It should be Hod Eller. I wish it was. Maybe it is. Maybe I should press forward and have Caine and O'Shea meet. Maybe now.

Deep into Chance's final season, way down in September, as the rain poured, he sat on the bench and waited for the game to be canceled. He had made two errors in the field the day before and had felt a tug in his hamstring while running out a hit. He was mortal. He would die. There was a stiffness in the joint of his big toe. His neck made a cracking noise when he turned his head. He was mortal. He would die. He was 40 years old, and it was time for the end. His marriage had been bad and was gone. His career had been glory and was going. Hurry up and rain this game out. Turn the outfield into a bog. Chance has the idea that he wants to go to the Museum of Modern Art. That is one good idea. Rain it out quickly. He should be there. If he doesn't get there, she will never know that he exists. Umpire Dill Baker walks out to home plate and waves his arms in a that's-it-forget-it-the game's cancelled manner. The remaining handful of spectators boo. The outfield is a bog. Caine is on his way to the museum.

✷ ✷ ✷

Nine years earlier in game one of THAT World Series:

Smiling managers Babcock and Byness shake hands for the camera. Randy Kepp, starting the game originally reserved for injured Lion ace Rainbow Clouds, blanks the Tigers, 4-0, thereby disappointing the Detroit crowd. Caine scores twice in front of Cliff Pinney home runs. Sepp and Caine turn 3 double plays and account for 18 of the 27 outs on defense.

✷ ✷ ✷

Kenyon Young was in that museum on that rainy day. Another piece of luck. The great ego pig of sports broadcasting was there to view the new photography exhibit, 'Homeless Depression Poor Starving Crazy Hopeless Broken Sad With An Occasional Ray Of Sunshine.' He was the catalyst. He introduced them. This is what he says happened:

"Did you know Chance Caine wore a rug? I bet not. He put it on when he left for the ball park and took it off after he got back to the hotel. Know why? So you folks out there wouldn't recognize him so much in his private life. Wore thin wire-rimmed glasses all the time, too, when he wasn't in his game disguise. Had perfect eyesight, of course. No lenses in the glasses. Just frames. I introduced him to the model O'Shea at the Museum of Modern Art in New York. I'd bumped into her earlier at the studio. I'd seen her at some parties before. A good looker, but not my style. Too lib. Worth a try, though. So when I saw her drifting alone and pausing to check out the daubs, I moved toward her to make a pitch. Well, I have interviewed Caine a number of times over the years for the great beast television, but I didn't know him at all away from the park. So I was semi-surprised to see him, complete with shiny bald head and wire-rim glass frames, standing in front of I think it was a Rothko. I had an idea. I don't know why. I thought it would be funny. I introduced them. I said, 'America's number one model, meet America's number one baseball player.'"

Nine years earlier, in game two: Six phoned death threats for various players of both teams are noted. Babcock's 20-game winner Simmons Dern beats the Lions 4-2 to even the Series at one game each. The big blow is a 2-run triple by Alfredo Escuela in the bottom of the eighth off of Lion reliever Father Frisch.

CHANCE

Her voice is low and strong. You want her to talk forever. She takes you for a magic ride when she speaks, and you do not want the ride to end. Chance Caine rolled a seven eight times in a row when he met O'Shea. This project's number one afternoon was spent listening to her talk into my recorder and eating really good big fat doughy chocolate chip cookies. Mmmmmmm, good. She described meeting Chance:

"What is this baseball? I thought to myself, if this shy little fellow is its number one player. I went to the game out of curiosity. I'd never noticed baseball before. My agent Dave Stebbet sat next to me to answer all my questions. He said he'd wanted to be Chance Caine all his life. How strange. The Chance Caine I saw at the Museum of Modern Art where that creep jerk Kenyon Young introduced us was hardly a mythic being. He was sweet. He talked about poetry. Well, you know, he smiled good. This is a mighty athlete? So I went to see him play."

Nine years earlier, in game three:
Nude triplets run onto the field and tackle the Lion

mascot during pregame antics. Babcock basks in warm 'homecoming' reception by the Lion fans and an 8-4 win to take a 2-1 lead in the Series.

The flash back, flash forward thing—please hang in there with it. It's not hard, and it's fun for the old bald guy, me. Now we go to Chance's green diary to find his reaction to being introduced to the woman he perceived as being his soul's mate. The book says:

> She melted my knees. That's about it. I turned around and saw her, and my knees melted. Oh, I have seen her in those perfume commercials on tv plenty. But in person, standing there, saying 'Hello', she was a melter of knees. Kenyon Young may be the biggest horse's ass in the continental United States, but I'll thank him forever for introducing me to Kathleen. Right away I was making a fool of myself spouting off about poetry and poetry of baseball and lahdeedah and yatahtah yatahtah. But she said she would come to the game if she could have a ticket for her agent so he could explain things to her. I said sure thing, and my heart did 9000 smiling pushups. I love her.

How a heart does a smiling pushup needs to be explained to me. But in game four, nine years earlier:

Kepp comes back, and he's still throwing ground balls. Lions win, 3-1. Caine is guilty of robbery three times, Sepp twice. Hulking Cliff Pinney lumbers into left center and picks one off his shoetops. As a matter of fact, nine years ago in game five: Simmons Dern is Babcock's boy. Tigers 5, Lions 2. Despite Caine's three doubles.

Dave Stebbet did go with O'Shea to the game. It was a gray day, but no rain. He told me, "O'Shea's a riot. Caine goes to the dirt behind second to get a low bullet, flips some amazing how to second for the force to end the inning and a bases loaded jam, and O'Shea says, "Was that good?' The whole stadium is up to its armpits in ecstacy and she says, 'Was that good?' After the game, I force her to take me to meet him. I played some short myself in high school. This guy's my idol. We are forty together. I slobber and babble a lot. He's a good guy. A damn nice guy! O'Shea says she liked the uniforms! Then she winks at him. Geez."

I know this woman. I can imagine something might definitely happen, concerning the solidity of your knees were she to wink at you. Nevertheless, nine years ago, game six was played:

Tigers need just one at home, but it isn't this one. Lions trail 6-0 after three, but scratch back, tie it in the ninth on Caine's 2-run double, win it in the tenth on Cliff Pinney's homer. "Father" Frisch works a three up three down ninth and a three up three down tenth.

They keep asking Flappy Byness. He keeps saying, "People have asked me time and time again why I didn't walk Red Pugh in the seventh game of the World Series with the Tigers when I had first base open. And I say because the game has to be won out there on the field. There's no way tomorrow can be turned into yesterday. Hearts were played out on both sides of the field, and ours were broken. What more can I say?" Without adding more, you mean, Flappy? Every year forever, game seven is played: Red Pugh's dream, Randy Kepp's nightmare.

CHANCE

Imagine the spokes of an old stagecoach wheel as train tracks. On each track, a locomotive is racing out of control toward the hub. Question. Could the hub be the waning days of Chance Caine's final season? Answer. Yes. Stay tuned. Don't touch that dial.

15

Image Drift

Name games. Playing games with names is something that I do. Look at this. I have chosen my All-Name pitching staff, and it boasts a starting quartet of Hod Eller, Eppa Rixey, Urban Shocker and Addie Joss. Those are names. From the bullpen I'm going to send Firpo Marberry at you. Look him up. He's there. I'll use Larry Sherry as a set up man and Chuck Churn as middle relief. Wow. I'm learning to sling these baseball terms around. Not bad for an old weird guy poet.

Tobe rhymes with robe Finley. Tobias Finley. Not Toby for short because Toby Finley doesn't work. Tobe

Finley. Tobe Finley is it. And Tobe Finley it was who managed against the most talented and superior Lion teams, battling them four years in succession to crash through to World Series Land. He said to me, "Who can forget it? Four years in a row we met Caine's Lions for the league championship. We won twice. They won twice. I doubt if there has ever been a better team than the one the Lions beat us with when we had our last battle for the National League spot in the World Series. Those Lions won 114 games in the regular season. Rainbow Clouds was at his absolute peak with 32 wins. Randy Kepp won 25! They had Caine, Sepp, Cable, Fenneman, Connell, Pinney—super defense and hitting to go with great pitching. But the key was 'Father' Frisch. He was the one element that had been missing from an otherwise perfect team. That year Frisch won 18 games himself and saved another 41. Funny, when Stony and Rainbow had their scuffle and Stony was sent packing, Frisch was racking up saves in Triple A. So Flappy Byness was the man standing in the right place at the right time when a big shiny ripe relief pitcher fell into his hand and made the Lions darn near unbeatable. It was one of the nutty oddities of life when Rainbow got his pitching hand smashed in his car door and missed the entire Lion-Tiger Series. Stony Babcock got his revenge, but it was sort of tainted by the absence of Clouds. What do you do with that Lion club at full strength? Bring on the '27 Yankees. I'd pay to watch, and my money would be on the Lions."

I steered him in the direction of an All-Star game he had managed at Wrigley Field, a game in which Chance Caine collected five hits in five at bats. I didn't have to use my cattle prod to make him bring forth, "Unforgettable. I can still see it. Having Chance Caine on my side! Hot dog! He gets five hits and makes about the same number of impossible plays in the field. He'd make a play, and the whole bench would come right up off their fannies. These are major league ballplayers. The All-Stars! And they're jumping up like nine-year olds! I looked around and noticed I was standing on my feet right next to them. Many a time Caine made this old infielder rise in disbelief at the plays he made out on that ball field. I managed the Pirates for nine years and had some fine clubs and players. But Caine's the best I ever saw. Period."

Academy Award. Short Documentary Feature. *The Fielder.* Filmmaker Jacques Michelle. How? Why? Talk, Jacques. Jacques talks, "I am not knowing much about the baseball when I have come down to be at Hollywood. My project before have been about the ballet. This is from where I am coming. The music. The dance. But this game on television, it catch my eye. The camera slow motion replay, it was Chance Caine taking the ball in a very beautiful movement. Perfect. He is dancer. So I take my camera with him around America and film the way he dance in this game. I put the music on top. Moonlight Sonata from Beethoven. It work like you see it like it is in my head. Chance Caine and me together, we have make good film."

Perfection. Perfect. That word keeps popping up when baseball people talk and the subject is Chance Caine. And now a camera jockey from Paris uses it, too. Three guesses what word Chance uses when he talks about *The Fielder* in his you-know-what-color diary:

> What an ego trip for me. That little Jacques Michelle, what an artist! It's perfect. It is a visual definition of why I love the game of baseball.
>
> I made a vow to myself after I saw it. I would not look at it again until my 65th birthday. I put the disc in my safe deposit box. I don't believe in living in the past. Turn the page. But I had to show it to Kathleen. I had to show her what I couldn't tell her about baseball and me. She

saw it and understood. She understands! Can she really believe in what I am? On the day I turn 65, I will watch the film again. If there is happiness, she will be there with me. What am I going to feel on that day 25 years away?"

Arthritis, maybe? Well, Chance Caine, if you have a 65th birthday, and on that day you do, for the first time, look back, you can't avoid seeing that last day of your final season, that day you are honored, that Chance Caine Day. Do you know that in the last few weeks of your final season that Verna Peckham is happy and pregnant in Illinois? Are you aware that Kathleen O'Shea is thinking, "To be beautiful is something, I suppose. I can build the mask. I have the face under control. My 'technique', my 'look', getting boring. I think Chance is my 'us.' I know it."

and

Rainbow: "The Rainbow possessed an unprecedented slider to complement his magnificent heater. And when the Rainbow added the Fortune Teller ball, so named because it crossed his palm with gold, the opposition was forced to hang their heads in shame and meekly accept the defeat the Rainbow would inevitably lay upon them. How did the Rainbow win game after game after game? Simple. He made them hit it to the shortstop."

and

Nelson Pick: "Angles, hand position, arm position, rotation, pull, snap, claw. The art of the force, the direction of the mind, all-consumed concentration, hit the spot from the optimum angle, bust his chops to protect that zone, fist him, front foot him, put the untouchable one from the angle to crease the corner, start him to thinking, don't give him any time or give him too much time, give him what he wants but not where he wants it, give him what he doesn't want right where he wants it, play him, cute him, nibble him, work him, be a smart pitcher."

and

In the last two weeks of your final season, Chance, Ben Blessee is preparing. He has been asked to speak on your Day. He will be at home plate in a purple checked sport coat and his voice will float out over Mander Stadium. Sure, Rainbow and Stony, Frisch and Pick, Connell, Philpott, you know, they'll all be there. Your old teammates will line up down the third base line. The present team will line up down the first base line. You will be at home plate, the point at the bottom of the V.

Lou Copter won't be there. He'll be somewhere else, out in the smoke.

⑯
The Fan

Before I tell you about The Fan, I've got to play another name game. Sorry about these little offshoots. But what can I say? That's the way it is. In this game, I build imaginary teams stocked with major leaguers having the same first name. I'm setting up a clash between the JohnJohnnys and the TomTommys. For the TomTommys I have Harper, Herr, Helms, Brookens, Satriano, Tresh, Davis, and Agee with Seaver, Greene, Boggs, and Phoebus working on the mound. Staring at them from across the field with cold appraising eyes from the JohnJohnny dugout will be Mize, Evers, Logan or Pesky, McGraw, Bench, Lowenstein, Briggs, and Callison with Tudor, Hiller, Podres, and Sain ticketed for duty on the hill. And wandering from one side of the field to the other, puzzled, confused, looking for direction from some higher authority, will be the lefthander with the rebuilt elbow, Tommy John.

Maybe there was a fan who saw every game the Lions played for 26 years. A life-long bachelor, thin and gawky, a seller of shoes in a fancy place, he lived alone in a rented room. He bought for himself a retirement present, a season ticket, box seat a bit beyond third base, for the Lion games. When the Lions went on the road and played, he was there, too, in the stands. Not being a spender of money, when he retired he had lots of it sitting there saved, and he spent it shadowing the Lions, observing them, for 26 years. He saw every game Chance Caine played.

After closing out the forty year segment of his life dedicated to the foot comfort of his customers, he had peered around for something new to do. He knew next to nothing about baseball, but began attending the games. "As a lark" he said. He found that he liked being out there—the noises, the green of the field, the way the pitchers contorted. He settled himself into comfortable rhythm. The taker of tickets adjusted his timepiece by the old man's arrival at entrance gate D. One Polish sausage, one bag of peanuts, one great big Pepsi on days that were hot. Substitute cocoa for the cool of the night. He built up a structure, a ritual frame. Peanuts in the second, Polish in the fourth, seventh inning stretch and a visit to the can. He spilled his drink once dodging a liner fouled off the end of Caine's two-toned bat. Over the years many high fouls off the bats of various left handed hitters drifted and fell near his place back of third. Just once did he get one to fall in his hand. Fenneman had raced and leaped at the rail, but the ball missed his glove by less than an inch. Instead, it bounced off reaching fingers and stuck out palms before lightly landing in the old man's lap. He kept the ball on the table next to his bed, under the spot on the wall where he taped the team's schedule.

On the road, he stayed in motels near the airports. He never did try to make personal contact with Lion players or ushers or fans. He just liked to sit there and look at the games. High up in Mander Stadium in the chandeliered opulence of the organization's heart, no one knew that the spindly old man in his eighties was the single sole witness, the one breathing person, who'd seen every game that Chance Caine had played in his major league life. They might have made a thing out of that, but they didn't know the man. This old guy kept tight to himself, not making noise or any commotion, looking around with his little bird eyes.

He liked the way he was spending his time. He saw them arrive, loudly or not. He saw them depart, whimper or bang. He saw miracle, comedy, tragedy, rage. He saw beauty, felt boredom. He saw youth turn to age, muscle to fat, phenoms go bust, stars rise and shine. And he tucked it away for himself, in his mind. And in his room in his bed he mulled it all over. And in his room in his bed one winter he died. And on opening day at entrance gate D, the ticket taker looked at his watch. "Old geezer's late. Musta croaked," he said.

Everett Mander sat up high in lush comfortable privacy and watched the games unfold below, a tiny tableau. Mander Stadium, clean, neat, and pleasant, possesses an around the clock all year long spring summer fall winter police security force to maintain unsullied serenity, safety and comfort of fan. Jumbo screened computer entertainment message board. White uniforms on the vendors of food. Lights in the night that gleam the green grass. Fireworks play in the sky.

Chance Caine met the model O'Shea. After that the green diary started to babble. In one spot, it says:

> Mander Stadium is more amusement park than strictly baseball stadium. That's why the fans come out to the tune of more than 4,000,000 a year. It is clean, pleasant, safe, and there is always a treasure chest of extraneous hoopla to keep the fans amused. Some of them even come to see the game. The fans in Chicago, New York, Philadelphia, Pittsburgh were always more appreciative of what was happening out there on the field when I played in front of them. But for the field itself, Mander is magic. Infield dirt a perfect texture to glide and dig in to. Bad hops are a rare species. Going back to track the high pop fly against the sky and settling there in the spot where it will fall down to me and I will take it. My place to patrol, my territory to defend, and I know it well. Someone else will walk out there next year. Good luck to him. I've had my time. Now I've got better things to do. Oh, yeah.

As Caine's last season rolled into its final weeks, Cliff Pinney of the Cubs, formerly of the Lions, was interviewed on a late night TV sportstalk show, He sent me the tape after I talked to him about the time his fist collided with Chance's eye. On the tape, he says, "When I went free agent, I came to the Cubs because they gave me first base. When we come in to play the Lions, I get a good welcome from the fans. They remember the ball club we had. It's a nice stadium to be in. That's the one thing. Mander takes care of it. I know Caine is hangin' it up. He was one hell of a ballplayer. I, for one, am going to miss seeing him out there. We weren't no friends as teammates, but that don't mean I don't think the man wasn't the best. Because he was. Shit, I'm almost through, too. Oops. Sorry about that."

In the last two weeks of your final season, Chance, you were falling in love. And Verna Peckham was pregnant in Illinois and Ben Blessee was preparing for Chance Caine Day and Stony Babcock was saying he'd be there locally and couldn't fail to attend his shortstop's day and Rainbow Clouds was making arrangements to leave his lagoon to be on hand and other people were circling the date on their calendars to witness Mander's party in honor of Chance.

17

The Love Thing

If a drop dead beauty from the end of the 18th century could fall for a one-armed, one-eyed sailor named Horatio, then why couldn't a drop dead 20th century beauty fall for an old bald shortstop? It could happen. It did.

I float comfortably on complete silence. I stretch out full length on my back in the grass behind the batting practice screen Eddie has set up behind shortstop and close my eyes and lie completely motionless for half an hour. Then I open my eyes, look at the sky, sit up, get up, focus in, get to the game temperament, get to the game. And when the game is over, it becomes difficult to step out of the clubhouse door and back into the world, the city, the street, the noise. Hard to be away from the game. This is what I will miss. Lying in the grass alone in the stadium.

What happened in front of that big square Rothko painting where they met in the museum? Chance didn't fall in love. He plummeted, then exploded, crashed, a sticky mess, in love. O'Shea? She found "the little fellow" amusing. But in a short space of time, she found herself able to say, "I have a spot where I can go along the California coast. The waves make a tremendous smashing on the rocks. I make my way to my special rock where I can stand and the white spray of a wave rises suddenly up in front of me and peaks over me before falling away. That spot is where I feel my strength, my harmony with all creation. It is a place to wash away the trivial, to contemplate being. I have never invited anyone along. It has been my private domain. Until now."

Years of fears build walls, and tiny things might trip them up. Tiny things gathered through the years of fears have the power to destroy in a puff of dust the reaching arms. What do you think of that? Love is a minefield and we know Chance made a wrong step once and blew himself to bits. The lady O'Shea has some heart scars, too. When Caine-O'Shea begins to bloom, there are guys around watching. Our friend, relief pitcher Carl Frisch, was there, and he ain't shy. Yes, ain't, ain't, ain't.

He says, "Women are better than men. They're not so hung up on sex unless they're, you know, screwed up mentally. I mean a normal woman has it more together in the knowledge of what's important and what's not worth shit, you know, in the general meaning of life and universe and all. An intelligent non-screwed up woman will be sensible and mature by her midtwenties. Whereas an intelligent, non-screwed up man will join the maturity party when he's forty or so. That's my theory. I thought about it when I saw Chance Caine acting like a 13-year old when he introduced me to this solid beauty O'Shea he had been seen with more than a little bit lately. You know, when we were out there in the bullpen talking about everybody else's business behind their backs, old Caine was a fertile subject. And, well, you know, some of us were semi-intelligent, and some of us were dumber than slime mold, but to a man all of us were under forty except Cranley, the bullpen coach, and he was not playing with even close to a full deck. So I listened to their claptrap sniggering about Caine and O'Shea, and I leaned back with a small smile, feeling superior. But at that point I am only 36 years old whether I like it or not, and I've got four more years of wondering first and foremost what this O'Shea is like in bed before I can move on to the contemplation of higher things."

There is a fashion photographer called Gouache, and he was happy to talk about O'Shea. This was not a surprise, as his name had topped the list of people to talk to handed to me by O'Shea herself. He had a curbside seat when the Caine-O'Shea fall in love circus parade was going by.

He remembered, "O'Shea, now this was a powerful centered woman from the first day I saw her. She couldn't have been, what, 19? She had class, style, look, poise, the whole package. A lot of things went right to produce that lady. She ranks right up there at the top for me as a working model. I used her every chance I got.

"Now she surprised me when she asked if she might bring a friend to observe a photo session we had scheduled. I do not like that at all. But when she told me the friend was Chance Caine, I said of course, bring him. I grew up in Chicago. I am of the species Cub fan. Now if you are of the species Cub fan, you are not a casual front-runner jump-on-the-bandwagon type. You have to love, know and appreciate the game of baseball for beauty, grace, drama, comedy. For things other than winning, to be more precise. I am an artist and a baseball fan. What other choice do I have but to hold Chance Caine up high as a symbol of art in sport?

"Well, she brought him. He was quiet, sturdy, moved slowly. Showed interest in the cameras and the work. You could see in a second that he absolutely adored her. And when we started to make pictures, well, listen, O'Shea rained passion on that man from all angles. For two hours. It went like ten minutes. Phhht. Afterwards, I felt as if I'd run a marathon. The atmosphere was electric, to put it mildly. After the two of them floated out, my assistant Felice turned to me and said, 'Wooowww!' I said, 'Exactly.' Those two have found what we are all here looking for."

Lucky them.

(18) Preparations

How does he stand the cold? Does he have a metabolism like one of those Tierra del Fuegan Indians early explorers ran across at the bottom of South America? Is he like John Muir with a packet of tea and one blanket walking the Sierra Nevada? Or Galen Clark, the wild bearded ancient who stalked the snowy Tuolumne winter barefoot? When I first tracked Lou Copter to his lair, he threw rocks at me to keep me a proper distance away. He still had a fairly strong and accurate arm. Later, after I had gradually talked myself closer, he allowed me to approach within conversational distance under a general cease-fire. I remained alert to possible attack and never turned my back to him. When the grooming goes, stay on your toes. There might be danger. Not inevitably, but conceivably.

I'm taking you to a December day not too far back. Cold foggy morning. How does he stand the cold? I stood at the window of my cheery warm den. Down there in the fog was the freeway underpass home of Lou Copter. In the spirit of the season, I dug out from my camping equipment a stained, smudged, wrinkled, but highly efficient, brown down mummy sleeping bag. After I had tamed it, my old brown companion kept me warm through many mountain chill nights. It had needed to be tamed because it had tried to kill me the first time I used it. You see, the zipper stuck. I was comfortably mummied in it and the zipper stuck. From a distance, I suppose, the twitching, gyrating, crazily flipping sleeping bag must have looked like a giant mutant pupa in a metamorphic panic. But it was only me trying to escape. I had the zipper replaced, and it never gave me a problem again.

The clerk at the store made a statement with his eyebrows when I bought six packages of SuzyQs. I left it unrebutted, walked back to my car, got in, and drove the overpass to the marshy side of the freeway. I parked where I could just make out the wooden post that marks the start of the jogging path. Off the path and up by the slough I walked, and when I got near, I called out his name. No answer in word or in flying debris. I leaned down. I could see better low, under the fog. I saw where the water disappeared into the darkness of the underpass. I called again and listened. Only traffic noise, cars and trucks, from above. I moved forward, holding the sleeping bag in front of me as a shield and the bag of SuzyQs dangling at my right hip. I drew closer and saw him standing there, a dark solid stillness in the moving mist. My breath was fog. I stepped forward, holding up the SuzyQs and speaking their name. He did not move. He stood there. Then I was close enough to hear his raspy breathing, and I reached out to touch him. At my touch, he leaped back, fell on the ground, began to moan. I knelt down and he looked straight into my eyes and mumbled. I put my ear close to his lips. He was saying, "I can steal it. I can make it. Hit one to the wall. Let me score standing. Make it easy. I can steal it. Make it easy . . . Make it easy."

I made the call for an ambulance from my car. I waited while they went and got him, brought him out, loaded him in, sirened off. I followed to the hospital where he died a few hours later in a nice warm room. How does he stand the cold? He doesn't. I showed up too late. From out of the smoke I came to him too late. Am I forgiven?

When Chance's final season was marching steadily through its last few weeks, Blessee began to spew in his column. Ben Blessee was spewing. He brought forth sweet cakey goo and smeared it under his byline.

Shortstop
by Ben Blessee

Honus Wagner, thick and powerful, was the first definition, in black and white, when the 20th century was young and the Kaiser made trouble in the world. Rangy ones Kerr, Marion, Banks, Belanger, Concepcion, waterbugs Rizzuto, Aparicio, PeeWee, the Captain, Smith, the Wizard of Ahhs. Then came Caine to stand above them all. And now the time for Caine to go approaches, looms, grows near. The 40th anniversary of his birth has passed, and yesterday I saw Chance err twice on ground balls and pull up lame running out a hit. Chance, good-bye. Good-bye, the thrill of the impossible made possible. Good-bye, deliverer in the clutch. The winning hit needed. You were there. The winning hit defended against. You were there. Write down the way you did everything, Chance, and you've written a textbook on how to play the game. What will you do, Chance Caine, now that you can no longer be Chance Caine? I salute you, Chance Caine. Thank you for 22 memorable years.

Chance Caine, Chance Caine, Chance Caine. Written down thusly three times in two sentences! Ben Blessee, take a deep breath. Relax. Get in the hot tub. Have a nice glass of wine. Chance wrote about you in his green diary:

> I can't believe the tripe Ben Blessee's writing about me now. My God, can this guy be serious? Senility got him early.

High in the sky at the top of Mander Stadium sat the owner in his sumptuous lounge. He thought about his business. It was a game. Business was a game. His grandfather had known how to play it. His grandfather had taught his father, and his father had taught him. The Lions are the family toy. The toy loses money. It draws 4 million customers a year. It still loses money. Look at the salaries. Preposterous. If he, Everett Mander, was there to make money, he wouldn't be there. He feels great affection for his ball team. He has said, "I feel a great affection for my ball team." It is his heritage and duty to the people of the community to provide them with the best possible team, whatever the cost in a monetary sense. The time comes to each player of the game when the reality of the end of the road must be faced. He loves Chance Caine like a son, but Caine is forty and he did make two errors in yesterday's game. The owner can't recall him ever doing that before. He tells himself that this game of baseball is a business. No room for sentiment. He can set Chance Caine up with a beautiful deal in the American League, where he could be a designated hitter for many more productive years. Caine has said that he would never be a designated hitter, but attitudes change when things have to be faced. There is a youngster in Triple A named Milius who is earning the highest marks at shortstop. Pearson says he will be ready next year. He adds that he looks like the new Chance Caine.

Everett, I wish I could have called Lester Carpens back from the dead to talk to you about 'a new Chance Caine.'

Lester, the scout who found and signed Chance Caine for the Lions, loved to talk baseball with his cronies. Even on his deathbed, he got great satisfaction telling the story of how he spotted and signed the great shortstop. To any soul who would listen, he would begin by saying, "There won't never be another Chance Caine. That's it. The end."

Now I am going to take you to the last several entries in Caine's green diary, presenting them numbered and in sequence. If you've got a problem with that, take it to the literature police. I'm in no mood to argue.

1. My divorce is okay. I got the house. She got the garden. She landscapes the place, sits by the pool, crawls around on her knees with her canvas gardening gloves digging, pulling, leaning back to wipe her brow and contemplate. Alice has the old green thumb, always had it. She makes good money landscaping in high income zones. The only thing she wanted in the divorce was unlimited access to the grounds to do with them whatever she wants whenever she wants. I'm going to give her the whole works, house and garden. Kathleen and I are going to build a new house somewhere magic. The season can't end fast enough for me. The dreaded moment the longtime ballplayer must face is here for me, and I can't wait to be history in this game. There's a new direction to go and a new partner to walk with. Let's do it!

2. Well, I suppose I deserve a Day if anyone does. When I told Mander I was retiring at the

end of the season, he nodded his nod that he always nods and told me he was expecting me to be back in the spring to help the youngsters, particularly Milius, to learn the game. I said thanks, but no thanks. I thought I'd cut myself off completely from the game for a while, at least. "Well, we are going to pay you tribute with a Chance Caine Day in our final home game this year." He droned on a while longer in his odd monotone. I shook his hand and left. September 30 is the day. A day of dread, a day of relief all wrapped up into one 24-hour package.

3. Disgusting, embarrassing. If I have to smile at any more gush, my face is going to lock on me. There's a lot of spouting going on. But the fans are great. They're with me. The cheers, the standing ovations tingle me, bring up the throat lump. 30 years I've been a short-stop, since I was 10 years old in Little League. Now I've come to the end of it, and the fans are telling me I've done it well. I'm lucky. What other people get buried in standing ovations of love when they close out their careers?

4. I had to be a liar to keep the nosey news guys out of my life. I've told Mander that I will

take his offer of a coaching job. I tell the scribes that I'm going to instruct infielders for Flappy and will probably be around as long as Stony Babcock. Seems to satisfy them. Except for Blessee. He shakes his head, sadly says, "It'll never be the same, will it, Chance?" Then he squeezes my neck. I play with him. Agree. Give him back a sad look. This guy hasn't got a clue. October 1, I am gone from this for good. Kathleen O'Shea has Irish eyes, and they are smiling for me.

5. Fall is the season of renewal for me. This one coming up more than ever. I pull on my spandex and run through autumn corridors of color. Run through those colors at sunrise or sunset when the air is chilled, and that's a good feeling for me. Spring running is okay. Winter running stinks, but still feels good when it's over. Fall, the changing of the leaves, that's the best time. That's where I get my religion, running in the autumn season. And that season is in her eyes. I can talk about love now. I'm in it. Love, I mean. Right smack dab in the middle of joy.

On the other hand, while he's sitting there in the middle of joy, numerous people are busying themselves with plans for his Day. Everett Mander announced, "What a wonderful honor it has been for me to be associated with the acknowledged master of our game of baseball, Chance Caine. In order to pay back in some small way for the countless thousands of thrills he has given to us and for the example of manhood he has always presented to our nation's youth, the Lions will hold Chance Caine Day on September 30th. Come out and join us in paying homage to this Hall of Fame human being."

Stony Babcock said. "I never was against burying the dead with the wounded when it comes to the fact that my old shortstop and who knows better than me he was the best of all our times is getting his Day and I wouldn't miss it even though my dainty feet will be feeling not the best to be stepping back into the Lions' den where I got thrown away earlier back then."

Everett Mander has a daughter. Sissy Mander will be trotted out on the Day to act as a kind of human yardstick to measure how long Chance Caine has been the Lion shortstop. She was born in May of Chance's rookie year. Chance played catch with her when she was a silent kid with a Lion cap pulled way down so she had to tilt her head back to see. On Chance Caine Day, she's a college graduate learning the ropes of the family baseball business.

But you aren't down to that Day yet, Chance. You're still saying good-bye to the opposition ball parks. Verna Peckham in Illinois bought two tickets for your last Wrigley Field game. One for her. One for her dad's ghost.

To see your farewell. The fans screaming every time you came up to bat or made a play. She was weak and crying the whole game. It ended, and the people all stood again, clapping, whistling, shouting your name. Her dad was there with her. She felt him hugging her so hard. And you came out once more and bowed, raised your arms out, then went away.

And once upon a time in the west, on the dry scrubby backside of the mountain, the Butterfield stage wound its bumpy way for California. Around the curve a tall rider in a long gray coat, masked, carrying a shotgun, waited. Driver threw down the reins and up his hands. The passengers stepped out, save one, who pulled his sixshooter from his army tunic and fired five shots into the bandit. The shotgun fell, went off, killed a horse. Highwayman slumped, slid to the ground. Ben Blessee's great grandfather Alfred had delivered justice with his pearl handled shooting iron. And Ben Blessee keeps the barrel shining and the pearl handle lustrous on display in his den.

And here's part of a letter that was written from O'Shea to Chance in that final season's final week.

"Love made a fool of me once and left me wounded. So I closed love away for a long time, lived glamorous, traveled the world. Now I think of a lifetime companion. Is it really you? I think yes. Strange, I never would have picked you out of a lineup. I was wary, peeking out from behind my defenses. Here you are, sweet with a gentle soul. A man who admits his imperfections and looks for beauty and meaning in the world. You loved me first. I was more cautious. But I find, to my amazement, that I love you. I look for happy, and with you, I find it."

CHANCE

two hearts joined
to race swift arrow
through the ever
together
as one

How long is the ever?

Where are the lies?

⑲

Hal Bennett

Although things seem to be careening along nicely down the track toward a collision with the climax of this story, being the cantankerous old fussbudget that I am, it's time to jump off the trolley, roll to the curb and stop. Get up, check for bruises, and walk into the mystery down an alley called

The Disappearance of Hal Bennett

I will tell you the story of Hal Bennett as I imagine Chance Caine lived it. I'm spinning you a tale. I lean back and call up the past.

It all began at a time in Chance's mid-career when the Lions trailed the Dodgers by three games as the race for the pennant headed into a September. And among the load of rookies to arrive on the scene and sit on the bench to watch the last month was a long, lean first baseman. His name was Hal Bennett. Down in Triple A he had hit 43 homers. He had thick wrists, plenty of muscle, and a whipping bat which sent high high towering drives over walls. Flappy inserted him into the cleanup spot to give limping John Cable a rest. Cable rested until the Lions reached the playoffs and would never have escaped resting if Bennett hadn't disappeared. This Bennett kid dropped into place in that lineup and into the tremendous pressure of a pennant race. On fire. He was on fire. He punished the ball. The Lions hopped on his back for the ride, and he carried them over and through the Dodgers to the division title. He was a shooting star of fame for one month.

And the first thing he said after his first game-winning homer was, "I'd like to thank you, Jackie Robinson, for killing yourself early to make it possible for me to be here." Chance Caine thought he was special, thought the kid had amazing maturity and poise. And when Bennett started beating Chance to the clubhouse before games, Chance Caine knew that Bennett was a once in a blue moon player. Chance said that in his opinion Bennett could have been the greatest home run hitter of all time. He had the power and the swing, and he knew how to get ready to play the Chance Caine way. There are other ways to get ready. Hal Bennett used Chance Caine's approach. Caine shared his almost empty ballpark with the rookie. The ability to focus was there. The Chance Caine way. Sure, there are other ways. But Chance Caine's way works. Who'll argue?

The Lions were at Mander Stadium on the last weekend of the season and needed one win to clinch the division. They got it on Hal Bennett's 17th and final home run of his major league career. Flappy put his arm around Caine in the clubhouse, poured champagne on his head. The ecstacy wound down to the point where the Lions could shower in the light happiness of success. Chance dressed, left the room, went outside, worked his way to his car, signing autographs as he went. He saw Hal Bennett in his own clot of admirers. He received a clenched fist victory salute from Bennett, returned it, got in his car and eased through the crowd and away. That was the last time he saw Hal Bennett. Bennett got into his car, drove off, and was never seen or heard from again. When Chance got to the park at 8:00 the next morning, he was surprised not to see Bennett there. So, he thought, we've got it wrapped up and he's going to let up on his concentration. Can't do that. Every game's the same, even the meaningless ones at the end, if he wants to be the best. He's got to learn that. But it didn't matter. Bennett never showed up. He had never made it home the previous day. He had last been seen leaving the stadium parking lot. Never found him. Never found his car. Vanished. Thin air variety. The Lions got swept in the playoffs. They couldn't concentrate. That's all. That's it. That's the end.

Really. Not only were the police baffled, but so were the tabloids. They had to turn to Carl "Father" Frisch to give them some ideas. They quoted Carl:

"I've got three, no, four theories on the Hal Bennett disappearance thing. You know, it took me five years in the minors before I got smart enough to develop my sidearm sinker and become a ground ball relief pitcher like they wanted. It took Bennett one season in triple A to step into the big time. The home run magic. There's your difference, you know. Anyway, obvious theory numero uno is that gamblers with heavy money elsewhere for the League Championships and the Series snuffed the youth's life spark. Number two is that Bennett had a deep dark secret in his past and it was about to surface, so he submerged and is still out there somewhere being somebody else, you know, and his fingers twitch when he passes the bat rack at his local sporting goods store, but he walks on by. Number three is he's making his way home and a UFO grabs him and his car in a ray and takes them up, up and away to some other galaxy so he can teach them how to take throws in the dirt around first base. Or finally, he might have made a deal with the devil, and after the Lions got to the division title, Satan came and collected him. There could be a musical in that one, you know."

When I asked Beece Brewkley, the southern gentleman Lion announcer, to talk to me about Hal Bennett, he nodded his head, took a sip of his bourbon and commenced:

"Well, sir, it has been my very great fortune to witness more than a few historical moments down through the years that I have been associated with this game of baseball. But I would have to say without a doubt that the most dramatic and unusual incident was the Hal Bennett phenomenon. In a nutshell, the Lions were in a terrific dogfight with the Dodgers as we turned into September. The rosters were expanded, and among those brought up from the minors was Hal Bennett. John Cable, the Lion first baseman, was limping around on a bad knee and Flappy Byness, the manager, decided to rest him. He planted young Bennett at first base and in the fourth position in the batting order, the power spot. Bennett proceeded to whack 17 home runs, and the Lions won the division, his final homer clinching it. The next day he was gone. He literally disappeared from the face of the earth. Not only did they never find a trace of him, but it turned out that after a little digging was done, there was no record of him ever existing before the day he showed up at a Lion tryout camp. Contemplate that for a while. Even so, for me, the tragedy is that we didn't get to see the young man play for ten, fifteen, twenty years. For he was a blossoming superhero. It became obvious the day he stepped into the lineup. He had the majestic power swing which made the fans buzz and ooohhh even when he swung and missed. And his home runs dusted the clouds. His outs entertained. And what's more, he was an articulate pleasure to interview. Composure? He had it as if he had invented it. This young man was destined to be a shining star to be gazed on in awe by the young fans. No doubt about it. Could not miss. But the Lord's plan was different. I don't know where Hal Bennett is today, whether he's dead or alive. I do know that he packed a career's worth of thrills into his one short month on the scene. And wherever he is, I would like to thank him for the image he left in my mind of a dedicated, talented, good-humored, friendly young man."

Okay. There's the story. I don't know. Dedicated, talented, good-humored, friendly. Could Hal Bennett have been from this planet? Let's see, what we have is

u n k n o w n	appears at tryout camp	single A to double A Triple A to Lions	v a n i s h	u n k n o w n

Rod Serling, where are you when I need you? You could do something with this Bennett stuff. I'd rather watch any "Twilight Zone" episode, especially the Agnes Moorehead one, than stare again at the tape of Kenyon Young interviewing Chance Caine after the retirement announcement had been made. But it must be done. We need a Chapter 20.

Do you remember Agnes bashing away at the little UFO with her broom? No? Your loss. That was a good show.

     a

      TV

        gem

(20) The Television Interview

commercial
commercial
commercial
another commercial and then

KENYON YOUNG   Chance Caine, a ballplayer for any
time, will retire on Sunday, September 30th. I have
coaxed him here to join me in today's "Spotlight On
Sport" to answer a few questions about his long love
affair with baseball and his imminent departure from
our national pastime. Chance, first of all, welcome.

CHANCE CAINE   Thank you, Kenyon.

KENYON YOUNG   The American public might be
interested in knowing a part of your personal story. Is it
true that your father was a college professor, a Ph.D?

CHANCE CAINE   That's true.

KENYON YOUNG   One wonders, then, logically,
    what were your father's thoughts when you opted to
    play professional baseball after your high school gradu-
    ation instead of enrolling at Princeton, where I under-
    stand you were going to play some basketball?

CHANCE CAINE   He didn't like it much, but he
    accepted it. He told me if my heart was in baseball,
    follow it. If I didn't make the grade, I could go to
    school later. He wanted me to live my life, not his life.

KENYON YOUNG   Well, you certainly did make the grade.
    But do you feel you might have missed something by
    not attending college, getting a degree, coming, as you
    do, from academically accomplished parents?

CHANCE CAINE   No.

KENYON YOUNG   Just no?

CHANCE CAINE   I've got a brain. I didn't put it out
    to pasture when I became a ballplayer. I grew up among
    college people. They're just people. No better, no worse
    than anybody else.

KENYON YOUNG   Of course, but that's not the point.

The point is that you are forty years old and facing the end of a 22-year long segment of your life with only a high school diploma and countless millions of dollars to fall back on. Others have gone before you, and a good number of them have not prospered, instead becoming pitiful used up relics who don't fit anywhere except in their own past glories. Chance Caine, can you handle life after baseball, Mr. Hall-of-Famer to be?

CHANCE CAINE   Oh, it's not all that dramatic, I don't think. I might muddle through.

KENYON YOUNG   That's quite a philosophy. Not bad for a 40-year old man, childless and divorced. Do you think if you heard about some man, a man 40 years old who lost his job after 22 years, his wife after 18 years and had no children, do you think you could call him a happy man?

CHANCE CAINE   You forgot about the countless millions to fall back on, Kenyon. Other than that, not your business.

KENYON YOUNG   I understand completely.

CHANCE CAINE   Well, that's good. Let me tell you the only things I think are pertinent in an interview. The toughest pitcher I ever faced was Rainbow Clouds in

spring training. I have loved playing baseball and regret
not a second of it. That's all you need to know.

KENYON YOUNG   Of course it is. Good luck to you,
    Chance. I'll be back in a minute with this week's
    "Stupid Plays." Stay tuned.

commercial about beer on an iceberg
commercial about cars on rocks
soap commercial, knockout blonde showering
    vigorously
happy hyperactive people quaffing sodas,
                        etc.

That sly boots Kenyon Young got Chance's dander up,
didn't he? Busted through the facade. Even made him tell
a lie. Chance, my boy, Rainbow Clouds was not the
toughest pitcher you ever faced. You lied. You'll never
forget Monkey Joe Huddleston and the brush of the ball
against your lips. You lied. You are a liar. Like me.

㉑

Man on the Street

QUESTION: WHAT DO YOU THINK OF CHANCE CAINE'S UPCOMING RETIREMENT?

AMOS BEECHER, RETIRED FLORIST: Retirement at forty. That's a privilege not a lot of people get. I hope he appreciates being paid millions for playing a game.

LINDA KART, TECHNOLOGICAL MAINTENANCE SUPERVISOR: The company has season box seats, so we get out to a lot of games. I've been going out to Mander Stadium since I was small going with my parents. Chance Caine was the shortstop the first time I went, and I'm 26 now and he's still the shortstop. It will seem wrong somehow to go out and someone else will be playing shortstop.

TOM TIBBIDIA, ADVOCATE: I wish the man well. I assume he will no doubt buy New Zealand and go live there if such a notion strikes him. He certainly has the cash.

DOUG FROWL, WAREHOUSEMAN: The pimp was an overrated bum. He was pure lucky. Sure, he could hit. So what? They say he was a great fielder. So what? He had the best pitchers you could ask for going for him. A lucky pimp who got all the breaks in the world. That's what I think of Chance Caine.

ROWDY BALLINGER, STUDENT: He was great. He was really the best. He was the best shortstop. He was really good.

SALLY DUNGENESS, MOTHER OF FOUR: Well, I'm not much of a football fan. So I don't know much about him. Is he important?

DONNA CANALLI, SALES CLERK: It's really sad. He's been there for so long. Since before I was born even. My favorite player is Fritz Fenneman, the third baseman. He's the cutest.

SCARAMOUCHE, PAINTED PAPER ARTIST: An era passes.

44 hits in 22 All-Star games. 70 League Championship Series hits. 42 hits in three World Series. 4305 regular season hits, so far. Eight batting titles and a career batting average of .335. A fielding average a shade over .993 for 22 years. More putouts, assists, double plays than anybody ever. Chance Caine? Never heard of him.

㉒

Chance Caine Day

An insane smelly former center fielder sitting on dirt by a weedy trickle under a freeway eating a SuzyQ once said to me, "I'm going to tell you something anyway. Some of the people in the hospitals are sick. Smoke all around them. They don't care, and they don't matter. Listen . . . it's the doctors. Keep it quiet. They got some powers. I've been keeping them off my trail. But I know some things that might matter. They might get you. A word of warning. Word of warning." His yellowy eyes glistened and water from them spilled down his sun-ravaged hairy face.

Blessee's column on Chance Caine Day was his usual spew. I have to put part of it here.

REMEMBER
by Ben Blessee

I looked down and saw a boy picking up ground balls in a manner unprecedented. A calm flame flickering to envelop the ball and snuff out instantly its progress. I saw this boy explode full bloom as the best ever from the opening day of his rookie campaign.

Magician with the glove, magician with the bat, he played the game with perfect skills. He played the game at full effort in every inning, and those innings piled up high in 22 seasons. And yet his team, at its best one of the greatest ever assembled, never came away from a season with the World Championship treasure.

And now we have reached the last day of his last season. Today we will honor him. Let it be a day that we all remember. Remember the day Chance Caine leaves the diamond for the last time. Remember what we will be losing. From this day forward, there will be only memories.

Among the many things he expressed opinions and theories about whenever I brought my poetic ear into his presence, Carl "Father" Frisch talked to me about the mental health of the people of this planet. His words fit here. They are: "Psychiatrists are, in a word, total and complete garbage dumps, sniffers of the cranial sludge.

You know, it's all a crock. They're as nuts as you and me. Nuttier! I got a theory about the hierarchy of lunacy. It starts at moderate loon and travels all the way to vegetable. And everybody on this world falls somewhere along the line between those two points. Everybody. You know it's a fact. Right? And I got a feeling the psychiatrists are leaning a bit more than heavily toward the veggie end of the spectrum."

A bowl filled with confetti. That's the blimp view of Mander Stadium on Chance Caine Day. Float down closer and you can hear the cheers and laughter at Stony Babcock's tribute die away in the fan packed oval. Beece Brewkley steps to the microphone, glances at his notes, and introduces Ben Blessee to speak. Blessee moves slowly forward and stands before the crowd. He leans into the microphone and says, "Ladies and gentlemen, boys and girls, today we will see perform for the last time on the field of play the greatest baseball player of all time. From the day I first saw him 22 years ago . . . And so on. References to Sultan of Swat, Georgia Peach, Columbia Lou, Stan the Man, Splendid Splinter, Ol' Diz, PeeWee, Scooter, Dutchman, The Hammer, Charlie Hustle, and more, more, more until he finishes. Then Blessee turns, draws his great grandfather's sixgun from beneath his checkerboard sport coat and fires five bullets into Chance Caine's body before he is wrestled to the ground by Rainbow Clouds and 74-year old Stony Babcock.

The doctors were amazed. It was not a difficult case. Caine must have been carrying a rabbit's foot. One of the witty doctors said that. Five bullets struck him, but not one of them did vital damage. They put some blood in him, patched him up and let his body do the healing. The Caine-O'Shea nuptials were celebrated in the hospital a week later. Chance was all bandages and smiles in an unofficial photo. The fake nurse who snapped the picture with a hidden camera was the star celeb among her tabloid cohorts for a few seconds.

Ben Blessee, right after the shooting, when he thought he was a successful murderer, talked. He said, "He had to go out on top. Look at Stony Babcock. He was an outstanding ballplayer in his time. Now he is a clown. He loves it, and clowns twice as hard to be noticed. Not for Chance. Not for Chance Caine to hit fungoes to the outfield. He cannot live with withered skills. I know him better than anyone. I found him. I discovered him. He must not live if he cannot be Chance, the ever young Chance making the unmakeable plays. I saved him the living death of growing old. I saved for this nation the untarnished image of Chance Caine, the best ever to pull on a pair of cleats and jog out to take possession of the territory between second and third."

When, one time a while back, I bought some SuzyQs and headed for the dwelling space of Lou Copter, he saw me approaching and yelled out, "Hey, come here. Let me ask you something? Is the smoke clearing yet?"

> charge a short hop
> pick it, flick it
> toward the reaching mitt
> the man is out
> he's out
> sit him down
> he can curse
> dash his helmet to the ground
> moan away to no avail
> the soft hand flicker
> oh so quick
> got him by a hair

epilogue

Twenty Years Later

In no particular order:

Flappy Byness is dead. He spent his last years directing minor league operations for the Lions. Some years earlier he had gone into a Floridian retirement. However, when his son Lloyd, who had married Sissy Mander, became president of the Lions after Everett Mander's death, Flappy came back into active service in the organization to work with his boy. Flappy's wife Yvonne lives on and treasures the poetic letters written to her by a smitten minor league infielder named Byness. He wrote to her once, "If the world was a deck of cards, you'd be the dove of hearts."

Stony Babcock lives. In the best nursing home that money can buy, he lies restricted to his bed. He managed Detroit until he was 70, then he was fired. What they called colorful at age 50, they called senility at age 70. So out he went, kicking and screaming, scratching and clawing. He was dressing for old-timer games well into his eighties. A lot of smiling heads gathered around him when the pictures were taken with the huge cake on his ninetieth birthday. He still breathes and mumbles, "You can say it all you want and I don't care, it's the fundamentals."

Red Pugh often sits in his basement den, a room filled with baseball memorabilia. Sits there in a chair facing a wall that is not a wall, but a giant blown up photograph, a photograph of Pugh captured in mid-ecstacy, head back leaping, and off to one side stands a Lion player, number 66 on his back, and to the other side, blurred in the background, walking away, is the pitcher Randy Kepp.

Randy Kepp is a high-powered attorney with numberless rich and famous sports stars as his clients. He has buried the memory in his successful legal career, but if it peeks out in the wee small hours at night, it can still twinge him.

Rainbow Clouds is an artist with acetylene torch and scrap metal. His constructions are installed and praised in various halls and malls throughout the world. His youngest daughter is Morning Mist, the model. Doors were opened to her by O'Shea. A vision of striking young beauty running at the water's edge was what O'Shea saw on her island honeymoon. The vision was Misty Cornell, and her fame was in the future. O'Shea saw it plain. And opened doors.

Bobby Ullett carries the mail no more. He drives his beat-up camper over the face of North America. Beside him sits Joyce, his wife, who thought she hated camping. She has discovered that she was mistaken. She loves it. It was camping with the kids that she hated. The kids are grown, married and away. So Joyce and Bobby roam, then come home to the California winter. Bobby has had two mild heart attacks.

Ben Blessee took his own life. Forget the details.

Kenyon Young on his 77th birthday married yet one more time again. "This way I got a 50-50 chance of remembering the anniversary" was his comment on his ninth entry into matrimony. He remains swine to the core and rich, rich, rich.

Henry Philpott, Caine's first second base partner, approaches 70 as a round smooth man with crinkly wrinkles at the edges of his eyes. He lives with his son, who is a member of the Congress of these here United States.

Beece Brewkley is a professional reminiscer. He will sit down and tell the stories, the triumphs and tragedies witnessed by himself traveling through a time frame that flashed alive with characters and incidents. He tells the stories well, and the listeners hang on every pause, every gesture. He is one who brings the old days to life and makes them sound better than they were. He lives in Sarasota, Florida.

Sister Sepp has been four times to drug rehabilitation centers. His body has quit him. His intelligence has not, but is straitjacketed forever. The honey doves no longer take care of him, but they do steal his money.

Lou Copter you know about.

Monkey Joe Huddleston, the fast, wild pitcher. Remember him? He travels to preach Eternal Salvation, crisscrossing rural America. He can make them stand and shout when from the pulpit he throws his body about and winds, kicks and fires his pitch for the Almighty God Our Father. He has welcomed thousands of sinners back into the fold with his long long outreaching arms.

The Lion, mascot of the Lions, hung up his claws at age 42 after saying to himself one day as he rolled around the infield of Mander Stadium chasing his tail, "What am I doing? I'm 42 years old!" He went back to college, became an elementary school teacher in southern Colorado.

Dr. Carl Frisch, yes, I said Dr., though well-liked and respected in the mountainous western community where he practices veterinary medicine, also puzzles the natives with some of his orations. Lately, however, he finds receptive ears when he spins out his theory on replacing the death penalty with surgical blinding. He reasons that there have been countless valuable contributing members of society who happened to be blind, and not too many of them had the ability to stick up a grocery store. "The way I see it, you could cut way back on guards and locks in prisons. You know, probably wouldn't even need prisons eventually. Right?" The men in the bar, relaxing after a hard week, nod. Makes sense, they think. Later, they decide all crimes of violence and all three-time losers be umbrellaed under the doctrine of pacificatory blindness, as it has been so named by Carl 'Father' Frisch, ex-major league relief pitcher.

Fritz Fenneman grows apples in his home state of Washington. Each spring he reports to Florida to prepare his Boston Red Sox for the upcoming season. Twelve years he has managed the Sox, and twice he has brought World Championships to Boston. His daughter Carla, named for a former teammate, is a first class ice skater and is training to win a spot on the Olympic team.

Bill 'Un' Able's Umpiring and Baseball Camp advertises:

KIDS 8-18 Internationally famous—Excellent facilities— Professional staff. PROGRAM: 2 weeks. Play in and umpire 6 to 8 games a week. Minimum 3 hours daily instruction. 5 diamonds—5 batting cages—5 training areas—video analysis. All kids learn fundamentals of playing and umpiring baseball for complete understanding of the game. ALSO: Fitness training, swimming, hiking in rugged coastal wilderness. Write:

> ABLE SCHOOL
> P.O. Box 420
> Lamb Shoal, CA

Alicerowe is what Chance's first wife calls herself now. She redid the grounds of the Caine and O'Shea hilly retreat after the big mudslide.

Chance Caine and Kathleen O'Shea remain united. James O'Shea Caine, their son, is about to enter Stanford to study anthropology. He skis and surfs. His 15-year-old sister, Mary Caine O'Shea, plays shortstop as a freshman on the high school softball team. She makes the plays. Her father coaches the team. Her Granny Nance watches and sees herself out there playing again.

Verna Peckham moved to Santa Monica, California before she gave birth to her son Artie. She works as a secretary in the UCLA Housing office. Her son, now a rangy 6'1" 19-year old, recently signed a contract to play professional baseball in the Lion system. Head scout Honey Brown recommended that the Lions draft Artie Peckham with their first pick, and Lloyd Byness agreed. Both men had watched the boy perform at Santa Monica Junior College. They had turned at the same moment to each other after Artie had flagged down a wicked shot up the middle and thrown the batter out. Brown said, "This guy reminds me of I-can't-even- say-it." Byness said.

"Chance Caine," Brown said.

"Yeah, he sure does."

Is this whole thing a pack of lies? Remember when I told you what a liar I am? Well, here's a fact. It is true that I was there in the room when Chance Caine spoke with Verna Peckham and shook hands for the first time with his son Artie. Why? Here's another fact. Though I am proud to be an old weird guy poet, I am proud to be something else, too. An ex-ballplayer. A member of the Hall of Fame. A shortstop. Yes.

THE END